Purple Daze

SHERRY SHAHAN

RP|TEENS
PHILADELPHIA · LONDON

"*Features snapshots of the turbulence of 1965 as caught in both a wide angle and telephoto lens. Perfect for short attention spans.*"

"*Part history, part teen survival, Shahan drops you into the Vietnam era with compelling authenticity and emotional force.*"

"*A raw and stunning portrait of the '60s.*"

Books published by Running Press are available at special discounts for bulk purchases in the United States by corporations, institutions, and other organizations. For more information, please contact the Special Markets Department at the Perseus Books Group, 2300 Chestnut Street, Suite 200, Philadelphia, PA 19103, or call (800) 810-4145, ext. 5000, or e-mail special.markets@perseusbooks.com.

ISBN: 978-0-7624-4071-9 (hardcover)
Library of Congress Control Number: 2010941249

ISBN 978-0-7624-4609-4 (paperback)
Library of Congress Control Number: 2012939191
E-book ISBN 978-0-7624-4247-8

9   8   7   6   5   4   3   2   1
Digit on the right indicates the number of this printing

Cover and interior design by Ryan Hayes
Edited by Kelli Chipponeri
Typography: Jezebel, Chronicle, and Gotham
Cover photograph: Copyright © Dennis Stock/Magnum Photos

Published by Running Press Teens
An Imprint of Running Press Book Publishers
A Member of the Perseus Books Group
2300 Chestnut Street
Philadelphia, PA 19103–4371

Visit us on the web!
www.runningpress.com

To Phillip Cole
... because you waited.

It's 1965

and
> The Sound of Music *wins*
> *the Academy Award for Best Picture*

and
> *President Johnson commits another*
> *50,000 troops to the war in Vietnam*

and
> *The Los Angeles Dodgers defeat*
> *the Minnesota Twins 4–3*
> *in the World Series*

and
> *Johnson increases the monthly*
> *draft call from 17,000 to 35,000*

and
> *The Righteous Brothers hit the*
> *charts with "Unchained Melody"*

and
> *Johnson says, "Nor will we bluster,*
> *bully or flaunt our power. But we will*
> *not surrender, nor will we retreat."*

and
> *Boys and girls play with fuzzy-haired*
> *Troll Dolls. Even Lady Bird Johnson*
> *has one.*

Ziggy

We're slumped on the front seat of a
low-slung Pontiac, cherry paint job.

Cheryl pokes the ashtray for butts,
finds the key. "Wanna go for a spin?"

"If we can be back by sixth period—
I did my homework."

I have the wheel in one hand, a Marlboro
in the other. We jerk down Ventura Boulevard
in second gear, and I'm yelling above Janis Joplin,
"Wait'll Mickey finds out we stole his car!"

Cheryl drums the dashboard laughing
because I don't have a learner's permit.

GRAND THEFT AUTO

That's what we tell the old guy we pick up
hitchhiking in front of Woolworth's.
He looks pale and asks us to pull over.

We couldn't stop now
even if we tried.

Mickey

So what if the guys joke about Ziggy.
Stacked. What a rack. Tight sweaters
look bitchin' on her.

She puts out too

even though her house has this choice view
of San Fernando Valley and her step-dad
plays in a band at Disneyland.

If I ever see a T-shirt that says,
SLUTS RULE, I'll buy it for her.

Ziggy

Guys like me because they
know I go all the way.

It's the only reason Mickey
takes me out.

Bet you didn't think I knew that.

Cheryl

The potato's been in the freezer overnight.
The Animals wail "We Gotta Get Out of This Place."
I pull a bottle of Sloe Gin from the cupboard,
hidden behind a box of Lucky Charms.

Ziggy cuts the potato in two,
carves Ziggy + Mickey into a half,
and makes an earlobe sandwich.
"Is this gonna hurt?"

I sip and dip the needle.
"Mine didn't even bleed."

The door bell rings, my next door neighbor.
I know his daughters, in fifth and sixth grade,
straight hair without ironing it.

Booze wafts through the screen door.

"What's up?" I ask.

His wing tips skim the WELCOME mat as he
lunges forward, slamming through the screen,
knocking my ninety-six pounds backward.

An old geezer with a tongue,
his hand on Don's senior pin.

"Cheryl?" Ziggy calls from the kitchen.
"Hurry up! My ear's freezing!"

Nancy

Ms. Hawes dresses like us:
Wool skirts. Mohair cardigans.
Sling-back flats. Seamless nylons,
nude.

Her skirts are minis.
But no one makes her kneel in the hall
to see if her hem touches the floor.

Here's another thing: Ms. Hawes uses a
blue pencil for corrections, never red, and
doesn't call on you unless your hand's raised.

There's a can of molasses on her desk. I saw
her in the cafeteria pouring it over fried potatoes
like Walter Cunningham in *To Kill a Mockingbird*.

When we read *Lord of the Flies* she passed a bag
of pork rinds.

Before beginning *Lolita* she brought in Cokes.
Cheryl throws up when Humbert Humbert
talks about sin, soul, and the tip of his tongue.

Weird.

Ziggy

Some numb-nuts poured strawberry
Jell-O in the toilet by the Girls'
Vice Principal's office.

She called the West Valley Police Station.
What if someone had slit her wrist or
had a miscarriage or something?

Talk about immature.

Get a boyfriend!

Cheryl

I finished *Lolita* in a bubble bath,
all three-hundred-thirty-six pages.

I cried
     and
         cried
             and
                 cried
                     and

.

   .

     .

Don

Dear Cheryl—

Today we have a substitute in Biology,
so I'm writing you a letter.

When you confide in your girlfriends
instead of me—I feel left out,
unimportant.

I know something's bugging you.

Why won't you talk to me?

I think our relationship is important—
that's why I want us to be *closer*,
if you get my drift.

     I love you very much!

   (For the 9,004,367,051st time)

I've never told another girl that I loved
her except K.S., and we were fourteen.

Love, Don

P.S. Guess who's captain of the golf team?
I'll get a bitchin' letter for my jacket.

Cheryl

Here's the thing:
my mom picks me up from school
when the nurse calls saying
I have men-stru-a-tion cramps.

She pays me for As on my
report card from the money
she saves by clipping coupons
and doesn't ground me
unless I ditch school
or sneak out at night.

I should tell her about our creepy
neighbor.

Crap!

Year Of The Snake

As Year of the Dragon gives way to Year of the Snake,
two squads of Viet Cong slice through a barbed wire
skirt at Camp Holloway's airstrip, sneaking in unseen,
one-arming satchel charges, blowing up helicopters
and reconnaissance air crafts.

Concurrently, guerrillas hiding 1,000 yards away poured
55-rounds from 81mm mortars into the compound.
52 billets are damaged. 7 Americans die. 100 plus wounded.

President Johnson addresses the National Security Council
around a casket-shaped table in the Cabinet Room,
responding to the slaughterous Communist attacks,
"I've had enough of this."

U.S. warplanes receive orders to destroy supply dumps,
communications systems, and guerrilla staging sites
north of the 17th parallel.

The White House states, "Whether or not this course can
be maintained lies with the North Vietnamese aggressors.
The key to the situation remains the cessation of infiltration
from North Viet Nam and the clear indication by the Hanoi
regime that it is prepared to cease aggression against its neighbors."

Nancy

Chatsworth High doesn't have
any Black kids.
Not one.

Angela, the girl who sits next to me
in biology, is Chicano. She eats lunch
with the Science Club, peanut butter
on Wonder.

Angela said if they bus in Negroes,
she'll transfer to another school.

"Why?" I asked her.

"They'd use our *toilets*," she said,
dissecting a frog.

Malcolm X

Born Malcolm Little, May 19, 1925, a preacher's son. Big Red, a teen involved in street crime. In prison by twenty, becoming Malcolm X six years later, spiritual desperado and controversial leader of black national movements.

February 21: Audubon Ballroom, New York

A crowd of 400 waits impatiently, curious newcomers and faithful followers. Tall and trim, striking in a dark suit, he walks purposefully to the lectern. Malcolm gazes into the audience amid a lengthy ovation:

"A salaam aleikum (Peace be unto you)."
They respond, "Wa aleikum salaam (And unto you, peace)."

In the dingy light, a man shouts, "Nigger! Get your hand outta my pockets!" A second diversion: a sock soaked in lighter fluid, flying fire. A smuggled-in sawed-off shot gun. A blast splinters the lectern. "Then all hell broke loose."

Malcolm falls backward, sprawled limply over a folding chair. His pregnant wife rushes forward. "They're killing my husband!" Men, women, and children flatten themselves on the floor. Others charge the assailants, kicking and beating them.

According to the medical examiner's preliminary autopsy, Malcolm X died from "multiple gunshot wounds." Two different caliber bullets and shotgun pellets.

February 27: Faith Temple Church of God in Christ, Harlem

Activist and actor Ossie Davis delivers the eulogy,

"Many will ask what Harlem finds to honor in this stormy, controversial and bold young captain . . . They will say he is of hate—a fanatic, a racist—who can only bring evil to the cause for which you struggle! And we will answer and say to them: Did you ever talk to Brother Malcolm?

"Did you ever touch him, or have him smile at you? Was he ever himself associated with violence or any public disturbance? . . . if you knew him, you would know why we must honor him. . . .

"Let his going from us serve only to bring us together, now. . . ."

—Buried as El-Hajj Malik El-Shabazz, Ferncliff Cemetery, Hartsdale, New York

Lysergic Acid Diethylamide

Chemist Augustus Owsley Stanley III concocts
his first batch of home-brewed LSD-25.

To control the quality, he tints each lot a different
color. Although the pills contain the same dose, myths
develop about attributes of the various colors.

Owsley is the primary acid supplier to Ken Kesey,
author of *One Flew Over the Cuckoo's Nest*, and
the Merry Pranksters—a band of communal friends
who trek cross-country in a psychedelic school bus
called *Further*.

February 21: Police raid Stanley's makeshift laboratory.
Not only does the errant apothecary beat the charges,
but he successfully sues for the recovery of his equipment.

Experts estimate the total production from his lab
at one-half kilogram or two million "hits."

Cheryl

Mom, do you have the late shift again?
Punching numbers into the cash register,
making change, bagging shampoo, toothpaste.

"Anything else, ma'am?"

rent
groceries
new tires

Will you be home soon?

My bag needs filling too.

Ziggy

Ms. Hawes gave every kid
in class a notebook. She
calls them *free* journals.

Our homework for the semester
is to fill the pages with *free* writing.

I love the word *free*.

Free-and-easy.
Free spirit.
Free love.

Only there're rules in all this freedom.
Pens. No pencils. No erasers.
No ink eradicator.

Once we put pen to paper we must
write nonstop for twenty minutes,

ink is like blood, smearing our
most private feelings across all
those clean white pages.

Freedom, I write, is not free if
strings are attached, even if it *is*
a homework assignment . . .

Cheryl

I love writing without thinking about commas or periods or spelling or being neat or worrying about anyone else reading how much I hate the creep next door and that I don't care if he was drunk because that isn't an excuse for sticking his tongue down my throat and besides I know he would have done more if he'd had the chance which is really sickening because I just about barf every time someone knocks on our door and I can't get rid of his disgusting booze taste no matter how long I brush my teeth and I hope his tongue got sliced up on my braces and writing like this makes me feel a little bit better because it's like throwing up when there's something bad inside so tomorrow I'm going to write more and the next day too until this sick feeling in my stomach goes away and then I'll write a thank-you note to Ms. Hawes because she gave us journals for free-writing and promised not to read them . . . .

Mickey

Dad substituted Jujubes for Jim Beam.
5 ½ days stone sober. Wiping out
his old record by 2 hours, 14 minutes.
That was when Mom split the first time.

This time it's Walter Cronkite's fault.

He fills a water glass, neat, no ice. I've seen
him like this before, no kidding, when he's
all fired up over the 6 o'clock news.

"Some things never change," he says,
as looters cart off sofas and Frigidaires.
A Magnavox is lifted from a burning building.
Magna-Color. Astro-Sonic Stereo.

From our 10-inch Zenith it looks like it's
snowing in L.A. Dad slaps at the rabbit ears,
knocking over the TV tray.

"Maybe we should go down there?" he says.
"Pick up a few things. You still got your
driver's license?"

He says this while watching
bottles, rocks, and bricks flying
upside down on our floor.

I grab my keys,
wishing I could
drive out of his life

forever.

Don

2:40 a.m.

Mickey has one hand on the suicide knob,
a can of Colt 45 in the other. Two wheels
hop the curb, taking out a fence.

Plunk. Plunk. Plunk.

Mick guns it down the 405 Freeway,
"You think Niggers bleed like us?"

"Black as tar!" I say.

Cheryl slugs me. "Shut up!"

I rub my arm, *What the hell?*
I was only kidding.

Lights slash the sky, like a world premiere
movie. Smoke's thicker too. Every ramp
downtown is barricaded.

I figure Cheryl wants me to tell Mick to ditch
the whole damn thing but he's going about a
hundred miles an hour and besides who knows
when we'll have another burn-baby-burn riot.

He doesn't slow down till we pass the 106th Street
exit where the National Guard stands on a ramp
with rifles, bayonets on their muzzles.

"Bitchin' uniforms," Mick says.
Then he punches it to the fast lane
and pulls over to take a wiz.

Bloody Sunday

Despite the Civil Rights Act of 1964, only 156
of the 15,156 blacks in Dallas County, Alabama
were registered to vote.

Revered Martin Luther King and 600 civil rights
demonstrators organized a nonviolent march from
Selma to Montgomery to protest discrimination and
intimidation preventing Selma's black population
from registering.

The peaceful protesters kneeled, prayed, crossed
the Pettus Bridge over the muddy Alabama River,
where they were attacked by state and local police:

tear gas
slap of billy clubs
snap of bones

Last month, twenty-seven year old Jimmie Lee Jackson,
farm worker and church deacon,
was shot in the stomach by a state trooper
while trying to protect his mother
and elderly grandfather when they were attacked.

Instead of being taken directly to the hospital,
where his wounds could have been treated,
Jackson was arrested, charged
with assault and battery.

Eight days later, Jimmie Lee died at
Good Samaritan Hospital in Selma.

—Bloody Sunday, March 7, 1965

"How Long, Not Long"

"Last Sunday, more than eight thousand of us started on a mighty walk from Selma, Alabama. We have walked through desolate valleys and across the trying hills. We have walked on meandering highways and rested our bodies on rocky byways. . . ."

". . . From Montgomery to Birmingham, from Birmingham to Selma, from Selma back to Montgomery, a trail wound in a circle long and often bloody, yet it has become a highway up from darkness. . . ."

". . . Our whole campaign in Alabama has been centered around the right to vote. In focusing the attention of the nation and the world today on the flagrant denial of the right to vote, we are exposing the very origin, the root cause, of racial segregation in the Southland. . . ."

". . . The bombing of our homes will not dissuade us. We are on the move now. The beating and killing of our clergymen and young people will not divert us. We are on the move now. . . . Like an idea whose time has come, not even the marching of mighty armies can halt us. We are moving to the land of freedom. . . ."

". . . Let us march on ballot boxes, march on ballot boxes until race-baiters disappear from the political arena . . . Let us march on ballot boxes until brotherhood becomes more than a meaningless word in an opening prayer, but the order of the day on every legislative agenda. . ."

". . . I know you are asking today, 'How long will it take?' Somebody's asking, 'How long will prejudice blind the visions of men, darken their understanding, and drive bright-eyed wisdom from her sacred throne?' I come to say to you this afternoon, however difficult the moment, however frustrating the hour, it will not be long, because 'truth crushed to earth will rise again.'"

"How long? Not long, because 'no lie can live forever.'"

—Public speech delivered by Dr. Martin Luther King, Jr., March 25, 1965 at the steps of the State Capitol, Montgomery, Alabama

Ziggy

I used to think about setting up
Daddy with Ms. Hawes, then
Bubba and I visited him last weekend,
first time in months.

1:30 a.m.

Cops gave him a lift from the hospital.
Frankenstein, a million stitches holding
his brains in.

Head-on with a power pole.

His girlfriend was pissed, locked herself
in the bedroom. Daddy passed out on the
couch, still loaded. Blood seeping through
gauze bandages.

Me and Bubba stayed up all night
watching his chest rise and fall,
wondering if he'd make it till breakfast.

Cheryl

Mom listened,
held me,

wiped my nose,
kissed my tears.

"It's not your fault.
It's not your fault.
It's not your fault."

Her voice warm
as my wound.

Nancy

The TV is full of stuff about rights.
Civil Rights. Employees' Rights.
Black Rights. Women's Rights.

Let's say I don't know the Girls' VP
went through my locker during Social Studies
while we watched news clips of Vietnam,
sickened by body bags.

Does that make it right?

From President Johnson

"Some 400 young men, born into an America that is bursting with opportunity and promise, have ended their lives, on Viet-Nam's steaming soil. . . .

"We fight because we must fight if we are to live in a world where every country can shape its own destiny. And only in such a world will our own freedom be finally secure. . . .

"Over this war—and all Asia—is another reality: the deepening shadow of Communist China. The rulers in Hanoi are urged on by Peking. This is a regime which has destroyed freedom in Tibet, which has attacked India, and has been condemned by the United Nations for aggression in Korea. . . .

"These countries of Southeast Asia are homes for millions of impoverished people. Each day these people rise at dawn and struggle through until the night to wrestle existence from the soil. They are often wracked by disease, plagued by hunger, and death comes at the early age of 40. . . .

"We must stay in Southeast Asia—as we did in Europe—in the words of the Bible: 'Hitherto shalt thou come, but no further. . . .'"

—Speech at Johns Hopkins University, April 7, 1965

Cheryl

2 a.m.

Blankets tucked around pillows.
Sen-Sens in my pocket.
Frosted lipstick, nude.

I open the window,
unlatch the screen,
crawl over the sill,
my heart a free-for-all.

The Blue Bomb is parked at the
top of the street. Brake released,
it rolls down.

Giggles spill out:
Ziggy and Mickey
Nancy and Phil
Me and Don

Mick pops the clutch.

Away we go.

Nancy

3:15 a.m.

Stopped at a red light.

Mickey yells, "Chinese fire drill!"

Mick, Don, and Phil tear around the
Bomb, climbing in on the passenger's side.
Now Ziggy's behind the wheel, trying
to steer with her boobs.

We fishtail through an intersection
of neon liquor stores, wrought iron
windows.

"Isn't Skid Row near here?" Ziggy says
while Phil nibbles my neck.

Mickey crushes his beer can,
"Fuckin' A!"

Ziggy

3:25 a.m.

Some scuzz shouts from a strip joint,
"Shake it—Don't break it!"

Cheryl clings to Don, scared, sorry she
came along. I cut lose with a shimmy,
forgetting Mickey has unhooked my bra.

Mick sneaks a peek in the door
under a flashing sign:

TOPLESS DANCERS
GLOW-IN-THE-DARK-TITS

Beer spills from a paper bag, while
Mick shoots the shit with a bouncer,
trying to convince him he's 21.

I bet those dancers make more than
the 50-cents an hour I get babysitting
psycho kid.

"Shake it, baby!"

Nancy

4:10 a.m.

Phil fumbles for my zipper.
I grab his hand, *no*.
My knees pressed together, *no*.

It's not like I worry about burning
in hell, like some goody-two-shoes.

It's not like I want to save myself for
my husband; I already know who he is,
Phil.

I imagine the not-you-too look on my
mom's face if another rabbit dies. When
hers died she got expelled from high school
and a shotgun wedding that keeps misfiring.

Cheryl

4:40 a.m.

I climb in, smelling like cigarettes
and beer. Hickey on my neck,
no doubt.

My knee bumps the dinner bell
tied to the shade. The hall light
flicks on.

Busted!

SDS

The first antiwar demonstration to receive
front-page exposure from the *New York Times*,
planned by an unknown organization,
Students for a Democratic Society.

Twenty-five thousand—beards, blue jeans,
ivy tweeds, the occasional clerical collar
marched on Washington, DC, singing.

Thousands bore antiwar signs:

Get Out! End The War! Peace!

—March on Washington, DC on April 17, 1965

Ziggy

In elementary school we memorized
"America the Beautiful" for Open House.

I sat in the top row of seats in the music room,
proud I knew all eight stanzas. After rehearsal,
our teacher called me outside, scolded me for
showing my underpants.

"From now on you will sit on the bottom tier
and cross your ankles like a proper young lady."

A helicopter hovered overhead. I thought,
*Channel 7 is here to report I wore my
days-of-the-week underwear out of order.*

Cheryl

Mom doesn't have many rules:

no boys in the house,
no cutting school,
no sneaking out at night.

I feel
bad,
sad,

but not because I got caught.

I want
to brush
Mom's hair
in front of the TV
and laugh
at Lucy
and Ethel.

Mickey

I'm just like you,
dear old dad.

No kids for me though. Why
put them through this shit?

My wallet's got fake IDs,
girls' phone numbers,
rubbers.

I'm set for anything!

Aren't you proud?

Nancy

Mickey and Ziggy stagger out of her
parents' bedroom. She's in cotton undies,
he's in skivvies. They're drunk as skunks.

He's holding her by the ankles,
36-D cups tied around his head,
a bra bandit.

She's upside down,
walking on her hands,
laughing like crazy.

I've seen them do this before
when the rubber breaks.
God knows why?
Bet she couldn't get pregnant
if she tried.

Ziggy

Feet in the air,
underpants up my crack,
boobs bouncing,

fat-tub-of-lard-upside-down.

If I got pregnant,
I wouldn't care
what anyone said.

If I got pregnant, Mickey and I
would spend the rest of our lives
loving our baby.

If . . .

Phil

Mick has no class,
treats Ziggy like trash.

I don't know why she
puts (out) up with it (him).

Suggestion Box Room 206

Can you open your room during lunch period, so we have a decent place to sit? (Not enough tables and chairs in the cafeteria.) I'd make sure no one put stinky food in your wastebasket or otherwise messed up the opportunity.

(Thanks for not making us sign our name)

Your outfits are quite hep for an English teacher. But, Ms. Hawes, I think you should try nude lipstick instead of pink. I also suggest a different eye shadow. Turquoise?

Your Fan

Who do you think you're kidding with this suggestion box crap? Teachers don't care what we think!

No Dummy

I wish you'd put the Hall Pass in a discreet spot so we don't have to raise our hand when we need to use the restroom.

Embarrassed

I like it that you read to us even though we're in high school. Okay so that's not a suggestion, but I thought you should know.

The Listener

I'd like to suggest that next semester you don't seat us by alphabetical order. I'm tired of the same "D" looking over my shoulder.

Serious Student

I'd like to petition that the bells ring closer together. Either that or blow up this dump.

Bored-to-Death

Sometimes a person is retarded due to circumstantial happenings beyond their control influence, such as missing the bus and having to pedestrian in shoes that crush obstruct their toes. If you have to mark us down (is it a school rule dictorium?) I'd appreciate the occasion to make up points. I don't dismiss book reports if you permiss us elucidation of comics.

Always Late

Cheryl

Ziggy can't surprise me, not
since second grade when she
beat up Michael Alan for calling
her Porky Pig.

The next day she let him touch her
scabby knee, and he shared graham
crackers and milk with her.

Selective Service System
Order To Report For Induction

IF YOU HAVE HAD PREVIOUS MILITARY SERVICE, OR ARE NOW A MEMBER OF THE NATIONAL GUARD OR A RESERVE COMPONENT OF THE ARMED FORCES, BRING EVIDENCE WITH YOU. IF YOU WEAR GLASSES, BRING THEM. IF MARRIED, BRING PROOF OF YOUR MARRIAGE. IF YOU HAVE ANY PHYSICAL OR MENTAL CONDITION WHICH, IN YOUR OPINION, MAY DISQUALIFY YOU FOR SERVICE IN THE ARMED FORCES, BRING A PHYSICIAN'S CERTIFICATE DESCRIBING THAT CONDITION, IF NOT ALREADY FURNISHED TO YOUR LOCAL BOARD.

Nancy

Phil got his draft notice.
I haven't told anyone.

MARINES

I tried to read it slowly,
but the words came all at once:

You are hereby ordered for induction into the
Armed Forces of the United States, and to report . . .

He took me to House of Pancakes.
I couldn't eat my Dutch Baby,
sobbing into his Union 76 shirt,
PHIL stitched over the pocket.

He smoked, drank black coffee
while I filled out a job application.

Phil

Man, those sneaky VC
fight dirty in Nam,
making a mockery
of U.S. democracy.

I'll be a proud *to be among the few,*
no better friend, no worse enemy,
first to fight, a gung-ho grunt
in the Marine Corps.

Cheryl

A Bekins van backs up next door as
I drag the sprinkler to a brown spot.

I'm guessing my mom told the creep's wife
what happened—and she booted the sex pervert.
I'm hoping she told him he'll never see his daughters
again, when

two mattresses are loaded into the van.
Twin headboards. Boxes, taped shut.
Barbie Doll suitcases, black, zippers open.
A pair of perfect faces peer out, plastic grins.

The hard-packed dirt beneath the brittle
grass sucks up water, trying to breathe.

Nancy

News time.

Walter Cronkite
reels a five-minute clip:

"Godless communism is why
we launch lethal weapons."

Boom. Boom.

National Liberation Front

For centuries peasants in South Vietnam accepted living in poverty because they believed it a punishment for crimes committed by their ancestors.

The National Liberation Front (NLF) seek to educate them in economics by explaining that 50% of the farmland is owned by less than 3% of the population. The NLF gains additional support by following strict directives:

> *Never damage the land and crops or spoil the houses*
> *and belongings of the people; never insist on buying*
> *or borrowing what the people are not willing to sell*
> *or lend; never speak to them in a way that is likely to*
> *make them feel they are held in contempt; assist*
> *them with daily work, such as harvesting, gathering*
> *firewood, fetching water, etc.*

The NLF begins confiscating property of large landowners and distributing it among the poor. In exchange, the peasants feed and hide soldiers and often take up arms to help liberate other villages.

If the U.S. Marines or Army of the Republic of Vietnam (ARVN) gains control of a village, they are told their land will be confiscated. Consequently, peasants think of the NLF as their friends and U.S. military and ARVN as enemies.

These beliefs are reinforced as explained by U.S. Marine William Ehrhart, "They'd (peasants) be beaten pretty badly, maybe tortured. Or they might be hauled off to jail, and God knows what happened to them. At the end of the day, the villagers would be turned loose. Their homes had been wrecked, their chickens killed, their rice confiscated—and if they weren't pro-Vietcong before we got there, they sure as hell were by the time we left."

Cheryl

Some girls put wadded up
toilet paper in their bras.
Mine has socks.

I mailed in the Free Trial coupon
in *Silver Screen* magazine under
a photograph of Jayne Mansfield.

BE A BUSTY BOMBSHELL IN JUST TWELVE WEEKS

When the package arrives there's
a tube of cream and a photograph
of a man's hand.

Mickey

Me and Ziggy swap spit at the drive-in,
an old flick called *Cat on a Hot Tin Roof*.

Don is in the backseat with Cheryl, moaning
like a sick animal, so I grab my squirt gun
to cool him off. He swears, totally pissed.
Cheryl just busts up.

Brick and Maggie sound like Mom and Dad
before Mom took off with that guy who sells
fake-leather encyclopedias.

I aim the gun in my mouth, all quiet like Brick.
"Nothing's gonna ruin my liquor."

Cheryl

Don tickles my tonsils with
Juicy Fruit and I wonder why

I can't be more like Ziggy
*   and less like me,*
letting him go all the way,

then Mickey blasts us with a
Screwdriver-filled squirt gun.

What a kick in the glass!

Don

Less than ten minutes
until the world blows its top.
I'm still a * _ _ _ _ * virgin.

Prayer For Peace

"On this Memorial Day, May 30, we will pay homage to our honored dead who gave their lives that this country might live in peace and freedom. Their numbers are legion, their deeds valorous, their memories hallowed.

"They fought in the valleys of Pennsylvania, in the trenches at Verdun, and in the foxholes at Guadalcanal. Now America's sons are again making the highest sacrifice to protect for this and future generations the liberty won in past struggles.

"Man possesses now the capacity to end war and preserve peace. We are able to eliminate poverty and share abundance, to overcome disease and illiteracy, and to bring to all our fellow citizens the fulfillment of their dream of a better life. We have the means to achieve these victories. . . .

"*Now, Therefore, I, Lyndon B. Johnson,* President of the United States of America, do hereby designate Memorial Day, Sunday, May 30, 1965, as a day of prayer for permanent peace, and I call upon the people of the Nation to pray for a lasting peace in which all mankind may reap the fruits of His blessing . . ."

—Lyndon B. Johnson, Memorial Day, 1965

FBI's Golden Record Club

The White House and Justice Department are aware that the FBI is conducting an "intelligence investigation" not a "criminal investigation" in an all-out war to discredit civil rights leader Dr. Martin Luther King, Jr.

Wiretaps in phones, in homes, and microphones hidden in hotel rooms to "obtain information" about "private activities of King and his advisors" to "completely discredit" them in a "personal attack without evidentiary support."

An FBI agent is dispatched to the Vatican to warn about the "likely embarrassment that may result if the Pope should grant Dr. King an audience."

The FBI responds to Dr. King's receipt of the Nobel Peace Prize by attempting to undermine his reception by foreign heads of state and American ambassadors in several countries he plans to visit.

The FBI prepares to promote someone "to assume the role of leadership of the Negro people when King has been completely discredited."

Ziggy

Today we saw the movie *PT 109* in
Social Studies class. Cliff Robertson
played John F. Kennedy in the Navy,
World War II.

I fell asleep and dreamed I was in the
White House, classy as Jackie before
Lee Harvey Oswald,

looking cool in silk taffeta.

Mickey

In kindergarten I had these plastic
army men.

I'd march them into the fireplace,
watching them melt into mutilated
green globs.

Dad laughed like crazy when he
saw them. "That's my boy!"

Think I'll drop out and enlist.
It'd be a blast to blow up stuff.

Ziggy

I picked up the extension when my
step-dad was on the phone, telling
my real dad horrible things about

me.

"Daddy never interrupted him.
Not once. Guess the whole world
is full of adults you can't

trust.

Rock 'n' Roll

Raggy rock and rollers whang electric guitars,
a sledgehammer rhythm on radios, rooftops,
stages, alleyways.

A raucous beat heaving patent leather feet
into discotheques from sea to shining sea:

Whisky A-Go-Go, California
Frisky A-Go-Go, Texas
Bin-Note A-Go-Go, New York

Parents barely survived
Pat Boone's white bucks
and Johnnie Ray's histrionics
when four Liverpool blokes took Ed Sullivan's stage
last year in high-heeled boots, shrinking suits,
and sufficient hair to stuff an easy chair.

"I Want to Hold Your Hand"

To distinguish themselves from the Fab Four,
the butch bluesy Rolling Stones are the band
"parents love to hate."

Mick's thick lips suggest how his nights are spent.

"(I Can't Get No) Satisfaction"

Teens rarely touch one another while dancing,
nor do they gaze into each other's eyes.
Yet psychiatrists and sociologists view
the orgiastic gyrations with horrification.

"Sick sex turned into a spectator sport."

A Senate subcommittee is formed to investigate
the link between rock 'n' roll and juvenile delinquency.

Cheryl

Six of us sway shoulder to shoulder
on a blanket a mile from the stage:
Don, Ziggy & Mick, Nancy & Phil.

A new band from San Francisco is playing,
Jefferson Airplane. Hazy pot smoke clouds
the park, but we're sipping cherry Cokes.

Ziggy dances in a stretchy halter top,
ankle bells keeping time to "Tobacco Road."
Mickey picks out rhythm on his guitar,
his strings solo singers.

Don and Nancy pay a visit to porta-potties
and Phil takes my hand, pulling me up.
"Wanna dance?"

"Okay," I say.

His smooth moves are easy to follow
unlike the boxy steps I remember
from fifth grade cotillion class.
"When did you learn this?"

We're palm to palm, a slow turn.
"My aunt teaches at Arthur Murray."

Another spin, I trip on the hem of my
fringed jeans, trying to laugh, except I'm
crying and can't stop.
"I don't want you to die."

He soaks up Signe Anderson, jazzy
in black leg-hugging leather boots.
"She sings like an angel."

I shout over her mournful voice,

"Tell them you're a pacifist.
Or flat-footed and a homosexual.
They don't take homos.

Oregon, Washington, *Canada*.
A thousand miles maybe?
You could make it in a day."

He kisses the tip of my sunburned nose.
"Sorry, honey. I'm not a traitorous wussy."

Nancy

Don bums a smoke from a guy with a
Pocahontas headband in a porta-potty line
that snakes like psychedelic dominoes under
a smoky green haze.

One flick and we all fall down, spreading
a runny egg of Communism:

South Vietnam and Southeast Asia,
before splashing across the Pacific until
America's democratic beaches turn red,
says the president and his shiny-starred
generals.

I've seen Phil fight when he thinks a guy's
putting the rush on me. But I can't imagine
him in a steamy jungle shooting at squat,
brown people in black pajamas, and

I can't imagine them shooting back.

I lose my balance and topple over,
another casualty of the domino theory.

Don

A country-rock band is on stage
warming up a banjo and washtub bass,
while I zigzag through a maze of
frizzy hair and peace signs:

MAKE LOVE, NOT WAR.

Good idea.

I spot Cheryl sitting cross-legged,
practically in Mick's lap. His shirt's off
and he's got his arms around her, his lecherous
fingers pressing hers to the guitar's neck.
He's wailing "Baby Love."

She smiles at me and blows on her fingers,
sore as usual from the steel strings.
"Mickey says I can keep it while he's gone."

I tell him to get up because I want to see
if the jerk has a boner and if he does, I'm
going to kick his zipper inside out, which
should help him sound more like Diana Ross.

He laughs hysterically. Like it's a joke.

Yeah, right.

Ziggy

History.

I've never taken such a hard test.

I read the True or False section first,
marking answers opposite to what I think
is right, so I'd have a chance of passing.

When I got to the Multiple Choice part,
I was so tired of not knowing the answers
I just scratched out letters.

All of the above.
None of the above.

I get an **F**.
Fuck.

Boot Camp

Drill Sergeant: "Your left!
                  Your left! Right! Left!
                  Your other left dickhead!
                  Sound Off!"

Platoon: "1-2"
Drill Sergeant: "Sound off!"
Platoon: "3-4"
Drill Sergeant: "Break it down!"
Platoon: "1-2-3-4-1-2—3-4!"

Drill Sergeant: "If I die in a combat zone,
                  Box me up and send me home.

                  Put me in a set of blues.
                  Comb my hair and shine my shoes.

                  Pin my medals on my chest.
                  Tell my mama I done my best.

                  Mama, Mama, don't you cry.
                  Marine Corps' motto 'Do or die.'"

Drill Sergeant: "Sound Off!"
Platoon: "1-2-3-4-1-2—3-4!"

Drill Sergeant: "Ain't no use in lookin' down.
                  Ain't no discharge on the ground.

                  Ain't no use in lookin' back.
                  Jody got your Cadillac.

                  Don't be sad and don't be blue.
                  Jody got your girlfriend too.

                  I used to date a Beauty Queen
                  Now I love my M-16!"

Drill Sergeant: "Sound Off . . . !"

Blackboard Room 206

Impromptu Writing: 100 words or less
Topic: Friendship
Due: End of Today's Class

MY BEST FRIEND

At first I thought what an easy assignment! Ziggy has been my best friend since elementary school. I can tell her anything, repeat *anything*. But when I started writing, all these feelings about my mom started coming out. I'm not going to put them down, because they're personal and I don't know if you plan to read these out loud. Since I have 48 words left, I will say this—I can count on my mom and that means a lot when you're a teenager.

—Cheryl

LONELINESS

Now that I've lived 17 years, I realize it's better not to let any one person get too close to you. That way you'll be used to being by yourself, so when real loneliness marches in to rip your heart out, you won't feel it.

—Nancy

FRIENDSHIP

I know lots of people, both in and out of school. But I wouldn't call them all friends. Bubba is more than my brother, because he listens to me like what I'm saying is important. That's an outstanding quality. Cheryl listens too. But even more than that, she understands when I get hysterical and wipes my tears when I cry. That should be in *Webster's* as a definition of best friend.

—Ziggy

Nancy

Phil's in Vietnam
in Jungle Fatigues.

I'm in an apron,
balancing plates of pancakes.

The old people order $2.49 specials,
short-stack, crispy bacon, black coffee.

I pocket sticky tips: Nickel and dime
my way to college.

Don

Dad's baking grass brownies for
tomorrow's march, while Mom
paints signs:

PEACE

The newspaper shows a police barricade:

TURN LEFT AND GET SHOT

My parents think they can walk the 45-mile
perimeter of "troubled activity" in downtown
without getting trapped in a crossfire.
Mom picked flowers for the cops.

They're nuts.

Cheryl

Thank god Don is still in high school so I don't have to worry about him getting drafted until after graduation and maybe by then the war will be over and all our soldiers will be home and marrying their girlfriends and moving into gingerbread houses and having kids and growing old together and dying in each other's arms and being buried in the same cherry-wood casket and more than anything I want this for Phil and Nancy and I promise to write Phil every day because some guys in Vietnam get lost in their minds and believe jungles and killing are the real world and forget what it's like back home and I don't want that to ever happen to him so I'm going to write about Boss Radio's Top 40 and *The Fugitive* tracking the one-armed man. . . .

Ziggy

Ms. Hawes asks us to come up
with ideas we'd like to research,
because she thinks we should spend
more time in the library.

"It doesn't have to be long," she says.
"Any ideas?"

Cheryl raises her hand. "How about
interesting quotes?"

Don nods. "Yeah, about war?"

Today we're peeling and eating roasted
chestnuts because we're reading Hemingway's
memoir *A Moveable Feast*.

Ms. Hawes talks with her mouth full.
"Can you be more specific?"

Nancy folds up in her chair.
"Is old guys dreaming up wars so
our brothers and boyfriends get shot
specific enough?"

Nancy

I'm teamed up with Don for the research project.
We meet at the library during lunch,
where he unearths a quote in a dusty book by
British historian, James Anthony Froude,

"Wild animals never kill for sport. Man is
the only one to whom the torture and death
of his fellow creature is amusing in itself."

The following day we wear black to school,
as planned. I have a fake bullet hole in my neck,
food-coloring blood spilling.

Ms. Hawes asks each pair to read in front
of the class. Ziggy and her partner chose one
by John le Carré,

"You should have died when I killed you."

Everyone laughs.

Me and Don are next. I found this one
myself,

"They wrote in the old days that it is sweet
and fitting to die for one's country. But in
a modern war, there is nothing sweet nor fitting
in your dying. You will die like a dog for no good
reason."

Ms. Hawes likes it because Hemingway served
in World War I, so he knows what he's talking
about.

I like it because the room is suddenly quiet
as a drawn-in breath.

Phil

Dear Cheryl,

5th Week in Hell

Thanks, doll
for the pics of roses—
I can almost smell them.

I'm lying on an army cot at my outpost.
Every breath, I suck in a battalion of bugs.
Damn insects. It's raining and they decided
to come in here where it's dry.

Last night I about got plugged writing
a letter using this same flashlight.

A sniper saw it.

That would be a helluva way to sign off—
with a big glob of guts.

Your friend, Phil

P.S. I got a nasty paper cut licking
the flap of Nancy's envelope.
Only one letter so far.
What's up?

Ziggy

Mrs. St. Johns faints in Home Economics
when she opens the refrigerator and sees
her Oscar Mayer wearing rubbers.

I mean, grow up!

Cheryl

Mom says I'm too young to shave my legs,
so I bought Nair. Industrial cream in a jar.

I'm not supposed to pluck my eyebrows either,
so I use her Lady Schick on the stubble between
my brows.

Ziggy says they're going to grow back thicker—
that if I keep shaving up there I'll have a mustache
between my eyes for the prom.

Napalm B

Simple bathtub chemistry concoction:

gasoline, noun. A colorless, liquid mixture of hydrocarbons, which evaporates and burns easily.

benzene, noun. A colorless liquid that vaporizes and is set on fire easily.

polystyrene, noun. A colorless plastic used for insulation and in making toys, household appliances, luggage, and reeds for musical instruments.

The Pentagon requests bids to manufacture Napalm from 17 U.S. companies. A small company in Michigan called Dow Chemical gets the contract. Before then, Dow was best known as the maker of Saran Wrap.

One 200-liter cylinder hitting the ground causes mass destruction. Flames roll in a circle approximately 250 feet in diameter. The heat inside the zone ranges from 1,800–3,600°F. Within the zone, there are no survivors.

Outside the zone, jellied gasoline clings to human skin, melting flesh. Reports document civilians being boiled to death in rivers heated by Napalm.

Don

Dad got cracked with a nightstick
during the protest. Seventeen stitches
in his scalp.

Mom calls from the emergency room
ticked because they weren't hauled off
to jail with their friends.

The doctor signed her petition, though,
so not all is lost.

Mom fixes Dad up on the couch
with an ice pack, puts on Dylan,
"Like A Rolling Stone."

Out come the brownies.

Phil

Dear Cheryl,

Let me tell you about a weapon
with a killing punch.

Howitzer: 109 mm. Weight: 27 tons.
Type of shells: White phosphorus.
Chemical. High explosive. Illumination.

Two weeks before I got here, a battery
killed 900 of the 1600 VC hit. Yesterday
two companies were sent to take a hill.
500 strong. Only 67 walked back.

Took the damn hill though.

Stay cool—Phil

P.S. I used to hate Disneyland.
Now it's all I think about.

Nancy

No one understands why I
volunteer for extra shifts at work.
Why I signed up for night class:
Psych 101.

Why I wasted tips and weekends
painting my bedroom *salmon*,
then bought a gallon of *raven*,
because all that fleshy-pink
left me too vulnerable.

Not much time to write.
Too much time to think
because shrapnel rockets
through my brain, ricocheting
off work, school, bone:

Is God going to spare P.F.C. Phillip
C. Rose because I want Him to?

Cheryl

Ziggy's been depressed since
Mickey enlisted in the Navy:

SEE THE WORLD &
DITCH YOUR DAD

She sobs into the phone,
"What if he gets sent to Nam?"

"Ships don't go to the
Demilitarized Zone," I say.
"It's on *land*."

She sniffles.
"If Bubba gets drafted,
he's flying the coop."

That's the first smart thing I've heard
her brother say.

Phil

Cheryl,

I've been awake for 42 hours.

I stood outpost last night.
The posts aren't sandbagged or fortified.
Just a shelter half-staked, so if it rains
you won't get too wet.

Mine's staked over a grave.

I hope those bastards smokin' pot and burnin'
their draft cards appreciate how hard it is peein'
in a bunker even when you're lying on your side
and there's a downhill slope.

The goddamn mosquitoes are having me for
a picnic, and we're out of knock-down spray.
I'll probably get Dengue Fever like the lieutenant.

Love, Phil

P.S. I don't tell Nancy the stuff I tell you.
She thinks I'm on some vacation
getting this bitchin' tan.

Nancy

I scribble in my journal, watering thoughts
and letting them sprout, like Ms. Hawes said.

All at once I'm outside, on my knees,
yanking weeds, tears turning dirt to mud.

> *I'm sorry, Phil, so sorry,*
> *it's an unbearable situation,*
> *and it's getting worse every second;*
> *the only way I can survive is . . .*

Before he left I swiped the bandana he
wore to the concert. It smells like his
coppery sweat and Lucky Strikes.

I knot it around an envelope, the
one with the Amelia Earhart stamp
I'm afraid to mail,
and slip them under my pillow,
sleeping with uncertain synapses.

Vietnam Service Medal

Established by Executive order 11231, signed by President Lyndon B. Johnson on July 8, 1965. To be eligible for award of the medal, individual must:

(a) Be attached to or regularly serve for one or more days with an organization participating in or directly supporting military operations; or

(b) Be attached to or regularly serve for one or more days aboard a naval vessel directly supporting military operations; or

(c) Actually participate as a crewmember in one or more aerial flights into airspace above Vietnam and continuous waters directly supporting military operations; or

(d) Serve on temporary duty for 30 consecutive days or 60 nonconsecutive days in Vietnam or contiguous areas, except that the time limit may be waived for personnel participating in actual combat operations.

In addition, personnel serving in Thailand, Laos, or Cambodia in direct support of operations in Vietnam during the same time period are eligible.

* Design created by sculptor Thomas Hudson Jones, former employee of the Army's Institute of Heraldry.

Ziggy

34 people died in the riots.
1,000 injured: 90 cops, 136 firemen,
10 guardsman, 23 people from government agencies,
773 civilians and protesters, including Don's dad.

I know because Bubba tore out newspaper articles:

TRAFFIC STOP SPARKS RIOTS
144-HOURS OF VIOLENCE
EIGHT MEN SLAIN: GUARD MOVES IN

118 of the injuries were from gun shot wounds.

What if Don had gone with his hippy dippy parents?

Don

I can't believe Kramer gave Ziggy
a B- on her essay about the riots. So
I stand up in class to make what I think
is a brilliant point:

"It's not kids out there killing, looting,
getting their heads busted open.

Hey, man, what's all this crap,

THE TROUBLE WITH YOUTH TODAY?"

Phil

Dear Cheryl,

I got my hair cut again today. Three of my
non-barber buddies gave it to me. WOW!
It looks like SHIT!!!

As far as whore houses go, they sure
as hell ain't government sponsored.
There is a whore for every GI here.
I don't know of a VC cooze
that won't go down for a buck.

Nancy needn't worry, though,
because they all have gonorrhea
or razor blades up their snatch.
It is the god's truth, too, because
a few guys in our outfit have
scars their moms will never see.

Your friend, Phil

P.S. Make sure Don gets married (you)
and has kids (yours) before he gets drafted.
I wouldn't wish this crap on my worst enemy.

Cheryl

Sluts wear red and black on Friday.
That's what Ziggy says.

I wear it for you-know-who,
though we don't go all the way

. . . yet.

Don

My parents signed us up for
an overnight retreat.
The brochure says we'll be
plunged into an environment
radically different from
our own.

It says, "we'll be taught by not knowing,"
whatever that means.

"You won't be alone, honey," Mom says.
"Several girls from your school volunteered."

Girls?

Ziggy

No problem getting a room
at the Aku-Aku for Mick's
going-away party.
Just wore a tube top.

Cheryl and Don are making out
on the bed. I'm in the bathroom,
smoking a joint, thinking,
I could be married to Mickey.

Picket fence. Station wagon.
Babies. Babies. Babies.

I ruin a tube of slut-red lipstick
writing a poem on the mirror.

Graveyards and headstones
    are merely a lie.
People never live
        therefore they can't die.

Instead of signing my name, I build
a Kleenex bonfire in the sink and

go blurry when white burns black.

Don

You think I'd spend the night at
the L.A. Mission if I'd known
guys are locked in one dorm,
girls in another.

Dinner: Greasy beans, macaroni,
stale bread, water.

Showers: Line up. Sign out towels.
Strip down. It's delousing night.

We're supposed to experience the many
sides of suffering. Dad keeps asking,
"What're *you* doing to relieve the pain?"

After stale doughnuts and watery coffee
we walk to Skid Row, twenty square blocks
of garbage, vomit, piss, and shit.

Dad takes Mom's hand, side-stepping
bums on the sidewalk. She teaches him
the words to "Gate of Sweet Nectar."

I duck into a diner for a burger, fries,
and chocolate shake. No way it should be
this hard to get laid.

Cheryl

His hot breath
in my ear.

Please move nearer.

His sweet lips
here, there.

I want you everywhere.

His whispers
inside and out.

This bra fastens in front.

A DJ on 93/KHJ AM
shouts into the motel room,
"Another hit from The Supremes!"

Our chaperones sing,

"Stop! In the Name of Love!"

Nancy

I drizzle syrup into glass pitchers,
fill salt and pepper shakers,
memorize Carl Jung for a test.

The psychiatrist smokes a pipe
beside my plate, *Adam and Eve on a Raft*.

The boss scrambles from the kitchen.
"Nan, there's been an accident—"

I choke on poached eggs on toast,
bump boysenberry syrup. Clots of
neurosis and disharmony
slop across Formica.

"Phil?"

"Oh, no, it's nothing like that.
It's your aunt."

I mop up the mess, confused.
My parents are only children,
like me.

"Your sister says it isn't serious,
but they need you at home."

It's got to be Ziggy hoping I'll go to
Mickey's party. I imagine them making-out
on a motel bed. God, I won't see Phil for
10 or 11 months.

By then I'll be in a state of malaise—
severed from all meaning of life.

Phil

Hey Angel,

It's been 14 days since I heard from Nancy,
so for the last few days I've been saving my
thoughts for you.

I'm at an outpost and so is a damn near-dead
Vietnamese farmer. He stepped on a land min
near his hut. Now his intestines are feeding fli

The choppers that are used for evacuation
are out picking up dead and wounded grunts
from a recon patrol ambushed 2 hours ago.

A marine came back with an ear tucked inside
an M&M wrapper, later speared it on the antenn
of his Jeep.

Life is cheap here—
right and wrong must
be talking to someone else.

I figure I should get a letter from you today.
Hope so.

Christ, I'm homesick, Phil

P.S. Am off on a nature hike—
all canopy, no light.

Ziggy

dear cheryl,

how'd your ortho appointment go? social studies was a **B-** on the scale of boring. kramer said we had to write an essay about flag-burning—and i wasn't really listening cuz it felt like one of my bra straps broke until he says torching a flag is a type of freedom of expression protected by the u.s. constitution—and sometimes people have to use more than their brains to argue for change in government policy—and it's up to people who know the difference between right and wrong to fight against authority—and it's sort of interesting so i sit up realizing my bra is definitely loose and i'm wondering who invented these boulder-holders—and he says there's no physical damage caused by burning a flag if you don't count ruining a good piece of cloth—and he's actually ranting about why tax payers should waste good money to prosecute pyros—and i'm thinking that bras should be burned too and how i'm gonna nab an **A** on this essay cuz he's got it all laid out until he says we have to write it from the opposite viewpoint—and then some numb nuts blurts out "you mean like burning President Johnson in effigy is the desperation of a deaf mute who can't find a more intelligent way to express himself?" i'm sunk.

love, ziggy

Mickey

USS *Hermitage LSD-34* Pussy Patrol

Don—

So, we snuck this dog on board for our
mascot. A scrawny mutt, probably a virgin.
We named him Stud.

The signalman flashed every ship
in the area till we found a bitch.

Stud got a bath and all gussied up with
aftershave. Everyone crammed in to
catch the action, but that bitch wasn't
interested in our guy.

I think she was a Lesbian.

"The Mick"

P.S. You better write if you want
to hear more of these true-life stories.

Cheryl

I learned to kiss in fourth grade.

Bonnie and I shared Harold,
her on one side,
me on the other.
We practiced after school,
like homework.

One day, Harold gave me a
Saint Christopher medal
wrapped in tin foil.

I still have it.

Mickey

USS *Hermitage LSD-34* Norfolk, Virginia

Dear Cheryl,

Guess what I had to do last night?

Wash everybody's sailor hat, I swear.
That's 80 hats. Took me 4 ½ hours.
Just because I didn't tell the CC
we were out of soap, no fooling.

God, I can't wait to get out of here.

Love, Mickey

P.S. Ziggy's letters are all the same.
If she doesn't stop asking about
"our future" I'm gonna dump her.

Don

Dad hasn't been baking as many
brownies since the price of a lid
(with seeds and stems)
hit ten bucks.

His new high is throwing himself
into L.A.'s low-life scum.

Every weekend he and Mom
stick a jug of water in a grocery
bag and grab IDs.

No soap.
No toothbrush.
No change of clothes.

"We can *tell* you endless stories about
people on the streets," Mom says.
"The point is, what are *we* doing to help them?"

Phil

Hi Doll,

Just changed pens. Mine's been
skipping for the last ten letters.
This one's Gunther's.

If we didn't have a mascot,
he'd be perfect—a big goofy gorilla
from Missouri who sleeps with his
fiancée's garter belt.

On pay day I left money on my bed,
and he put it in my locker.
We never steal from each other—
just from the company next door,
mops and brooms.

I'll never take electricity for granted again.
Guess that's true of a lot of things.
I'm so horny I can hardly put my hat on.

I have 7,360 hours more to serve till I get leave.

Your friend and a bit more—Phil

P.S. I'm so bugged about no mail from Nancy
that I halfway wish I'd get shot up bad
enough to get sent home.

Mickey

USS *Hermitage LSD-34* Miami, Florida

Dear Cheryl,

We're getting underway for five months.

Listen to this:
South America, Panama, Jamaica, Trinidad,
Puerto Rico, Guantanamo Bay.

There's more, but I can't remember them.

Sorry I messed up on the tape recorder.
Next time I'll use a slower speed so I don't
sound like Alvin and the Chipmunks.

Love, Mick

P.S. Can you look up Cuba in Kramer's atlas?
I'm a little lost.

Cheryl

Don slams the brakes,
too late.

We stall
on a ledge, a
steel teeter-totter.

Pedal to the metal;
back tires spit dirt.

We start walking,
his arm on my shoulder,
street lights winking below.

My heart slows, wishing he'd say
he loves me before we find a pay phone
and call a tow truck.

I'm dying to say it back.

Don

Dad bursts in with the *Los Angeles Times*.
"What happened to the Rambler!"

White walls muddy,
weeds in tail pipe,
broken hood ornament.

"Hell, I don't know," I say,
sinking a carpet putt.
"You must've gotten high
last night, driven off a cliff."

That stops him real quick.

Mickey

USS *Hermitage LSD-34* Philadelphia, Pennsylvania

Dear Cheryl,

They are definitely working us.

Today I lugged 200 lb. barrels of oil
up and down ladders from the bow
to the stern of the ship.

The next two weeks we are going out
all day to shoot. I'm kind of worried
cuz the last time we went out to shoot,
I lost part of my hearing, no shit.

When I get home I'm going to throw a
3-weeker like you've never seen, I swear.
I have an ID card that says I'm 21. We'll
have a supply of booze that won't quit.

Love, Mickey

P.S. I'm saving for a Swinger so
I can send you some pics.
Can you send me some?
I miss my peeps.

Phil

Hey Cheryl,

Let's start out with what I did today:

5:00 a.m., firing off the guy.
6:00 I hit chow (stale toast and raw bacon).
7:30 our work day began.

10:00 me and Gunther worked with ammo.
10:30 we switched from coffee to beer,
which always improves our mood.
12:00 we ate hot chow in mermite cans.

1:00 we cleaned the gun. Gunther cleaned
the muzzle break—I cleaned the breech block.
All that bullshit was finished by 3:30.

I am pissed right now because this is the
6th day since I didn't get one single letter.
Got a damned bill though, forwarded from
the telephone company.

Missing everyone, Phil

P.S. Did you hear about the bed-wetting Klansman
who went to his meeting in a rubber sheet?

Mickey

USS *Hermitage LSD-34* Lost at Sea

Dear Cheryl,

Does Don feel like a big man with his pot?

That bastard still hasn't written. It's a shame, too.
I've got so much stuff to tell him. Stuff you just
can't tell a girl.

I went to New York last weekend. I got
drunk on top of the Empire State Building
with a girl.

We threw paper planes off it.

Love, Mickey

P.S. I still have 9 letters to write tonight.
Ziggy won't be one of them.
P.I.S.S. Has she lost any weight?

Ziggy

My first word wasn't
Momma or Dadda like most kids.

Bubba,
because I couldn't say brother.

Hey, Bubba?
It's still just you and me!

Suggestion Box Room 206

I didn't put a note in the box before because I thought it was a big joke.
But I noticed the Hall Pass is now kept in an envelope by the door. Can we
get a pencil sharpener that doesn't break off the lead?

Believer

Maybe we could trade clothes sometime?

Your Fan

I *suggest* you use this box for a piñata.

No Dummy

I like all animals because they don't yell at you or tell you what to do.
Maybe we could have a class pet? A gerbil or snake?

The Listener

Can we change seats after mid-terms?

Serious Student

Here Lies Bored-to-Death

Thanks with particular gratefulness for allowing extra credit due to the
circumstantial occurrence of my parents late-nocturnal-shift employment, which necessitated babysitting chaperone duties over my youngest
sibling. I absorbed your library suggestion and savored the drawings
depictions of sheeps as homo sapiens even if it wasn't a comic book.

Always Late

Phil

Hi Doll,

I get $20 every 15 days. I put $10
in my wallet for the 30-day leave
I'll have when I get out of here.
The other $10 is for smokes and beer.

Beer is only 15 cents a can
and most of the time it's free.
Schlitz or Pabst Blue Ribbon.
Does the job though.

What has the Navy done for Mickey?
They say the service changes everyone.
One thing for sure, Nam is changing me.
I've never been so goddamn horny in my whole life.

Luv ya, Phil

P.S. I'll be a Lance Corporal soon.
P.P.S. I'll drink an extra beer for you tonight.
P.P.P.S. Maybe I should send Nancy some USO
stationery and a few pens.

Nancy

* Love, a losing game
  One I wish I never played
  Gamblers never win

* Haiku: Ms. Hawes's class

Mickey

USS *Hermitage LSD-34* Puerto Rico

Dear Cheryl,

One of the guys wants to write
a couple of lines for the hell of it:

Hey Babe,
I would very much like to take you
out when we are on the West Coast.
Mickey has told me all about you and I
think we could have a nice time together.

It will be sometime in April
so save a date for me o.k.?
Well, guess I've said enough
so here's Mickey.

P.S. Be sure and save a kiss for me.

His name is Teague but we call him
Narcissus. If you don't know who
that is look it up in Greek mythology.
He's from Texas and all.

Please don't listen to the Mick because
I'm not really conceited because
conceit is a fault and I have no faults.

He said to say that he's really good-looking.
Sad isn't it?

Love, Mickey

P.S. Thanks for the fudge.

Phil

Hi Cheryl,

How are things?

I'm sitting in my hole,
trying to stay awake,
wondering where the war is.

I've learned two things:
Never take off your boots
unless you're showering.
Never turn in your M-16 once
it's drawn from the armory.

Well, I ain't visited a shower in days.
Think I'll risk it. Gunther has hotel soap from
his leave in Thailand. It smells like pretty girls,
warm feelings.

As always _____ _____ !!! Phil

P.S. Marines requisition about anything,
even Kotex. Great bandages, helmet pads,
slathering BBQ sauce on pigs.

Ziggy

Another Colt-45 goes on the pyramid
in the corner of Bubba's living room.
Bet there's a thousand of them stacked
on each other, aluminum acrobats.

Bubba opens a tidy roll of wax paper,
pinches dried green stuff,
sprinkles it on a Zig Zag,
rolls it smooth,
twists the ends.
"Wanna try some?"

"Why not?"

Being a good brother,
he talks me through the steps,
even though I've seen him smoke endless joints.

I focus on the red-glow tip, choking
back fried apple pies from McDonald's.

"Far out."

Bubba tickles me till I pee my pants.

Phil

Dear Cheryl,

There are two types of warriors here,
classified by drugs.

Drunks destruct in alcohol, fighting among themselves.
Potheads rely on marijuana, peaceful and agreeable.

You can tell a Head by their smokes.
Never flip-top boxes. Always soft packs,
opened from the bottom.
A carton of Kools, $2.50.

Mama San skillfully rolls each cigarette
between her palms—tobacco tumbles—
replacing with high-grade marijuana.

The *new* cigarettes are tapped back in their packs.
Each one stacked in its carton. All for $10. A $12.50
investment yields 200 mentholated marijuana cigarettes.

I carry a pack in my shirt pocket,
lighting up here, there, everywhere.

Miss you, Phil

P.S. Don't believe Johnson when he says
counterinsurgency in the countryside
is winning the "hearts and minds"
of peasants. Bullshit!

Mickey

USS *Hermitage LSD-34* Pussy Patrol

Don—

Last week we landed on this small island.
The native women were topless. Man, you
should've heard the cheers from our ship!

So the damned chaplain passed out Navy T-shirts.
Here's the kicker:

the women cut holes in front for their tits,
no shit.

"The Mick"

P.S. Did you know Cheryl writes really bitchin' letters?
Let me know if you aren't gonna write, so I can
stop wasting government stationery.

Ziggy

I wrote Ms. Hawes a note so she'd know we
learned the difference between *lie* and *lay*
in elementary school—that the stupid questions
about chickens getting *laid* are from jerk-offs.

I scribbled the who's-your-best-friend essay
with a busted pencil because that's all I had.
Ms. Hawes didn't make me copy it over in ink.

She's the only teacher who makes me feel like a
real person. Most of the teachers here haven't
bothered to learn my name.

Phil

Hey there, Cheryl,

I love your letters about what's happening
back there, especially the homey little phrases.

I'm enclosing a shot of myself behind a
50-caliber machine gun. This machine killed
13 VC 3 nights ago.

We drink beer constantly and most of the time
we're half lit. If I quit drinking it'll be because
I stopped a bullet.

I can shave my arm with my knife without a nick.
That 6-inch blade is sharper than any razor.

Later—Phil

P.S. I sure miss the sweet aroma of my mom
frying bacon on a Sunday morning.

Mickey

USS *Hermitage LSD-34* Non-Virgin Islands

Dear Cheryl,

Congratulations on your grades and all. If
everybody keeps up their grades maybe our
crowd will make something of their selves.

Next week we're going to Jamaica.
They have legalized prostitution there.
I'm not the type to buy it, but betcha I do.

I won $28 playing cards last night,
no kidding.

Love, Mickey

P.S. I fell asleep on the flight deck for 2 hours
and have the most bitchin' tan on my face.

Cheryl

Don said we should invite Ziggy to see the new Beatles movie *Help!* because it's supposed to be funny and Ziggy could stand cheering up which I know better than anyone so I don't say anything when she squirts Sloe Gin out her nose wrecking my new paisley hip-huggers in a laughing spasm because Ringo gets a sacrificial ring stuck on his finger and a couple of bumbling scientists named Professor Foot and Algernon chase the Beatles from Buckingham Palace to Switzerland and I think the story is stupid even though John said something cool in an interview about getting loaded while making the movie, "we were smoking marijuana for breakfast . . . and nobody could communicate with us because it was just four glazed eyes giggling" and then I think about Phil and wonder if he gets a chance to laugh between crouching in paddies and giving Juicy Fruit to Vietnamese kids with missing limbs and just about that time Ziggy pukes in a box of buttered popcorn and I tell Don it's time to go.

Phil

Hey Sexy,

As far as a Navy guy in your wallet, a shot of a
Zipperhead would be an improvement. We might
not be as bright and shiny as the squids, but
ground pounders are more proud of their grime
than squids are of their shine.

As far as taking care of myself, don't worry.
4 dead buddies before breakfast is enough to make
anyone careful. The 4th guy caught a sniper round
in his chest during a fire mission.

We emptied his pockets:
pack of smokes, Black Jack gum,
an envelope postmarked Baton Rouge.
Dropped everything with the twisted dog tags
in a plastic bag and looped it around his wrist.

Me and Gunther wear AK47 Rounds as necklaces,
gook protection. Slipped rubbers over our rifle muzzles
to keep out rain. Can shoot through 'em.

Hell, I shouldn't be writing about this stuff.

Phil

P.S. The radio is playing something about dudes
named McGuinn and McGuire who couldn't
get no higher. Nice tune.

Cheryl

Ziggy leans against my locker:

> "Wanna cut class? My
> brother's across the street."

I say, "Kramer's giving a test."

> "Like I care."

"I studied till two."

> "One zero. It'll average in."

"I get paid for As."

Ziggy pops NoDoz and Sleep-Eze.

"Mick would have a fit if he saw you."

> "Who's going to tell him?"

Not me.

> "No one gets it. Enlisting was
> like sleeping with some girl."

I get it, Ziggy.

House Of Representatives

Mr. Bray (Republican, Indiana) speaks to a proposed bill adding 4 words to the Selective Service law "knowingly destroys, knowingly mutilates" referring to draft registration and classification cards that all men in the United States between the ages of 18 and 35 are required to obtain and keep in their possession:

"The need for this legislation is clear. Beatniks and so-called 'campus-cults' have been publicly burning their draft cards to demonstrate their contempt for the United States and our resistance to Communist takeovers . . . Just yesterday such a mob attacking the United States and praising the Vietcong attempted to march on the Capitol but were prevented by the police from forcibly moving into our Chambers. They were led by a Yale University professor. They were generally a filthy, sleazy beatnik gang . . . This proposed legislation to make it illegal to knowingly destroy or mutilate a draft card is only one step in bringing some legal control over those who would destroy American freedom."

—The bill was brought to a vote and passed the House by 393 to 1 with 40 not voting on August 13, 1965.

—President Johnson signed the Bill into law on August 30, 1965.

Mickey

USS *Hermitage LSD-34* Guantanamo Bay

Dear Cheryl,

I'm here in Cuba soaking up the sun.
The base is 45 square miles. Just like a city.
Civilians live in it and all that junk.

I'm standing watch on the back of the ship.

If I see anyone swimming it's my job to find
out who they are and if they don't answer up
I'm suppose to fire a shot in the water near them.

If they still don't answer up I swear to god
I'm suppose to shoot to kill. This is an enemy
country. The base is only leased to us.

So far I haven't killed anybody.

Love, Mickey

P.S. The cookies you sent were mostly crumbs
but the guys still appreciated them.

Phil

Dear Cheryl,

Did you know it's possible to have
110% humidity without rain? It's so hot
I sweat salt through my flak jacket,
which makes it heavier than the usual
6 pounds, 6 ounces.

I had this revelation and slit the bottom
of the nylon shell, ripping out 6 pounds
of Kevlar-type fiber.

My helmet is a steel pot, about 5 pounds.
Peace sign scrawled on one side. I put the
camouflage cover over the lightweight liner,
dumped the pot. Nothing can slow me down;
I got it dicked.

Can you believe Gunther dressed up for Halloween?
Somehow he scrounged a red Santa suit.

No "Ho! Ho! Ho!" though.
He shouted, "Trick or Treat.
Smell my feet.
Give me something good to eat."
The guy looked like a big, fat,
fur-trimmed blister.

Guess the jungle was fresh out of candy canes,
cuz he passed out grenades, pins straightened
for easy lobbing.

Love, Phil

P.S. Are you seriously considering going to
nursing school after graduation?
You can take my temperature anytime!

Cheryl

Mom hardly dates
    since Daddy died.

Now there's this guy,
    seems nice enough.

He picks her up on Friday nights,
    brings me Nuts & Chews.

Mom wears lipstick and sling-back heels.
    "It's a real date."

I say it's okay to invite him over
    for English muffin pizzas
      and *The Beverly Hillbillies.*

Will he sit by her on the couch,
    hold her hand like Daddy

While I eat my Nuts & Chews?

Mickey

USS *Hermitage LSD-34* Guantanamo Bay

Dear Cheryl,

QUESTION TIME:

No, I never shot anyone swimming in the water.
It's a good thing I didn't get the chance because
I don't know how to work the gun, swear to Buddha.

No, I didn't spend all the money I won playing cards.
I still have 33 cents left.

I definitely got some P***Y in Jamaica.
That slays me.

Love, Mickey

P.S. Ziggy hasn't written much lately—
probably too stoned to hold a pen.

Phil

Dearest Cheryl,

I'm sitting in my tent listening to the monsoon
winds and rain ruin everything—including our
morale, which is lower than a cockroach in hell.

Zipperheads fight more fiercely in the rain.
Paddy algae, jungle rot, spongy mold
communicate in code. Damn leeches.
Just chopped up one with my bayonet.

Today we were supposed to go on operations
down south. Now there's a 5 day delay.
We smoke.
Drink Kool-Aid.
No one talks.
Not even Gunther's bullshit to chew on.

Man, I wish I could take in a drive-in movie. See,
the trouble is, we don't get any saltpeter in here.
In the 10 months since I left, I'll probably turn into
the worst sex maniac to ever hit L.A.

Love, Phil

P.S. I started writing this letter on a box.
    Now I'm sitting in it. Damn thing broke.

Cheryl

The girl who shares my PE locker traded
tight sweaters for Empire-waist dresses.
Gym shorts tugged over a girdle.

One Saturday her boyfriend drove her to Tijuana.
Monday she returned to school,
tight skirt, no girdle.

Ziggy used a coat-hanger
in a gas station bathroom,
nearly bleeding to death.

Mickey doesn't have a clue.

Mickey

USS *Hermitage LSD-34* Pussy Patrol

Don—

I thought we were friends, man.
But you're too goddamned busy
to write one lousy letter.

If you could spare a few minutes,
I could tell you about all the bitchin'
babes I've met.

There's one good thing about the Navy
(two if you count all the pussy)
and that's I don't have to listen to my
old man anymore.

He does write some damn decent letters though.
But I wish he'd stop asking about medals, like
he's keeping score or something.

Your ex-friend,

"The Mick"

P.S. I hope you rot in hell with double-boogies.

Ziggy

Everyone here's asleep so I call Bubba,
listening to his stupid phone ring
off the stupid hook,
unraveling threads on my cutoffs.

I suck a roach on the porch,
holding everything in.
Maybe if I get high enough
I can quiet my head;
maybe then I can blink
without seeing Mick's flat-top,
velvet freckles, his peachy skin.

Damn it, I'm thinking about him again,
little heartbeat bombs.

My bare feet collect street grit,
counting the steps to Don's house
three blocks away.

I tap on his window,
choking on smoky giggles.
"Wake up!"

He's angular behind the glass like one
of Golden Dragon's fortune cookies.

"Can I come in? It's *freezing* out here!"

Mickey

USS *Hermitage LSD-34* Guantanamo Bay

Dear Cheryl,

I don't think Don would lose respect
for you if you went all the way with him.
But just between you and me,
I wouldn't do it.

I don't care what he or anybody says.
If he went all the way with you he would
definitely have the urge to brag.

All it would take is for him to tell one
guy and you would be screwed
in more ways than one,
if you know what I mean.

Make him marry you first.

Love, Mickey

P.S. Tell Ziggy she's got 90 days
to get to 110 pounds.

Ziggy

The	Fire
Between	My
Thighs	Cries
For	Mick
My	Heart
Tick	Tock
Has	Stopped
Without	Him
There	Is
No	We
No	Me
No	. . .

Cheryl

"WHY'D YOU DO IT?"
"It's not like I love her."
"I KNOW, IT WAS JUST SEX."
"She tapped on my window."
"YOU DIDN'T HAVE TO OPEN IT."
"She was stoned."
"SHE'S MY BEST FRIEND—*WAS*."
"I don't love her, Cheryl."
"I'LL NEVER FORGIVE YOU!"

Don

Cheryl,

I don't know how it happened—
me and Ziggy.

I promise to pay more attention
to what my dick is thinking,

if only you'll forgive and forget.

I love you!

Ziggy

Sometimes I think about that girl,
sixteen and still in Jr. High,
a greaser transferred from East L.A.
Razor blades in her hair.
Camels taped to her binder.
Black eyeliner,
thick as licorice whips.

She didn't talk to anyone but me.
Maybe she thought we weren't so different.
Bubba liked the black-blue ink x
she needled under her skin.

I like the idea of razor blades.

Cheryl

No one's home so I put *West Side Story*
on the stereo.

The Rambler pulls into the driveway, the hood
ornament at half-mast. I pull down the shades,
lock the door, crank the volume.

"A boy like that wants one thing only,
And when he's done he'll leave you lonely."

I

leap
lunge
plunge
               l
sweat   f   y
                i   g!
                   n

Phil

Dear Cheryl,

Our troop carrier breaks down so me and Gunther
thumb a ride on a rag-top tanker with a zippered
back window. FTA painted on the guy's helmet,
Fuck **T**he **A**rmy. We figure he's hauling water
to some remote outpost.

Man, his rig's tuff. An M-16 hangs on a windshield
"T" handle, muzzle down. The metal plate on the dash—
advisories on how to maintain your vehicle,
in case the driver forgot—holds grenades:
6 frags, 2 smoke, 2 white phosphorus.

A radio is the headrest behind his seat,
tuned to the armed forces network.
A 3-gallon jug of Kool-Aid with cup inside,
a cooler on the floor, full of Pabst.

You can tell this guy knows the road—
can tell he'd spot a new divot from
exploding devices.

I ask about the hole in his door. "Lucky bullet," he
says, caressing the wheel. "This truck'll never let me
down. It's true love, man."

"What're you haulin'?" Gunther asks,
dipping Kool-Aid.

"Fuel."

Gunther just about shits his pants.
"This here's a fuckin' 5,000-gallon
Molotov Cocktail. Pull over, dude,
we'd rather walk."

Love ya, Phil

P.S. Spent my 20th birthday in a bar listening to
"I Got You Babe" with a Vietnamese accent.

International Day of Protest

October 15, 1965. After lunch at the Catholic Worker, David Miller takes the IRT to the Armed Forces Induction Center in lower Manhattan. Police barricades line the streets, separating war protesters from hecklers.

Dressed in a dark pinstripe suit, a white button-down shirt, narrow tie, and short hair, David climbs a ladder onto the platform of a sound truck. "I am not going to give my prepared speech," he says, pulling his draft card and a book of matches from his pocket.

One match, then another blows out in the breeze. Someone offers him a lighter. David raises the burning card as a group of Hare Krishna chant, "My Sweet Lord," dropping it when flames singe his fingers.

Three days later David Miller becomes the first activist arrested under the new Selective Service law for "knowingly destroying" his draft card. The FBI apprehends him at St. Anselm's College in New Hampshire where he's talking to students about pacifism and universal peace.

Ho Chi Minh Trail

For centuries, this trail meandered through sparsely
populated jungle, facilitating trade in Southeast Asia
a basketry of truck crossings, river systems, primeval paths.

Barefoot hordes drove oxcarts and heavily-laden bicycles,
human pack animals.

1959 Armed conflicts escalate between the National
Liberation Front (NLF), also called Viet Cong,
and the first president of the Republic of Vietnam,
Ngo Dinh Diem.

1961 The People's Army of Vietnam works on
the trail and the use of motor transports escalates.

1965 The trail develops into an intricate network:
dirt roads peppered with supply bunkers, barracks,
hospitals, control facilities, and tunnels: hard-packed,
underground living areas with field hospitals and
command centers.

Motto: Build roads to advance.
             Fight the enemy to travel.

Mickey

USS *Hermitage LSD-34* Pussy Patrol

Don,

Now that it's daylight savings I can start playing
golf after I knock off ship's work. With some luck
I might get on the ship's team.

I don't like to think about what I'm going to do
when I get out of here—besides throw a bitchin' party.

Guess I'll take the GED. If I don't pass
I'll be the oldest guy in high school.

I'm sending you a fag from Tortola,
but that's it, man,
I swear!

Your ex-friend,

"The Mick"

P.S. Cheryl said you might bag that
assistant pro job at the country club.
Prick!

Phil

Hi Gorgeous,

Five days of nonstop rain and I'm sick
of watching my yo-yo walk-the-dog,
tossing cards into my helmet,
sharpening my Kabar blade,
so I started translating the *Olyhay Iblebay*
(Holy Bible) into Pig Latin:

Inay ethay eginningbay, Odgay
eatedcray ethay eavenhay anday earthay.

That's *Enesisgay*. 1:1.

Love, Phil

P.S. Did you really break up with Don?

Mickey

USS *Hermitage LSD-34* San Juan, Puerto Rico

Dear Cheryl,

HICKORY, DICKORY, DOCK.
TWO MICE RAN UP THE CLOCK.
THE CLOCK STRUCK ONE,
BUT THE OTHER ESCAPED
WITH MINOR INJURIES.

WHAT'S RED AND SITS IN A CORNER?

Hold up to mirror:

SEDALBROZAR GNIWANG YBAB A

I didn't write all the stuff I thought
to write about but I guess this will do.

Love, Mickey

P.S. The cords to "Nowhere Man" are
hard to play if you don't use bar cords,
especially in E flat (E$_b$).

Cheryl

The needle sticks on "A Boy Like That" and his *I love you but I slept with your best friend* doesn't mesh with my idea of love, so I grab a pen holding it like a dagger over my journal, slashing the page into confetti and ripping it out and wadding it up and tossing it in the toilet and flushing and starting over, writing to Don, telling him how much I hate him and how he branded my heart and that I'll never forgive him for what he did, not ever, and then I drop it in the toilet and pee all over him.

Don

Hello again—

I'm home now and can't stop
thinking about you, about us.

I've told you I love you many times,
and I truly mean it, even if I'm not
so hot at showing you.

I know you don't want to talk to me
right now. But maybe you could write
a letter and give it to Nancy?

Things could be perfect, Cheryl,
if you'd give us a second chance.

All my love, Don

P.S. I miss you!!!
P.P.S. I'm sorry!!!

Ziggy

* I'm lipstick
  nail polish
  mascara.

  A short squat
  package people
  buy without
  looking inside.

* Free Verse: Ms. Hawes's class

Cheryl

* HATE HATE HATE HATE HATE
  HATE HATE HATE HATE HATE HATE HATE
  I HATE DONALD DUCK

* Haiku: Ms. Hawes's class

Norman Morrison

(December 29, 1933–November 2, 1965)

A devout Quaker and father of three young children pours kerosene over his head and sets himself on fire outside Secretary of Defense Robert McNamara's office at the Pentagon in an act of self-sacrifice to protest United States involvement in the Vietnam War.

Mickey

USS *Hermitage LSD-34* Puerto Rico

Dear Cheryl,

Guess what?

I got relieved of one of my jobs.
Guide Bearer. My CO said (quote),
"What in the hell makes you think
you can laugh at everything?
This is the Navy!"

Me, "I know, Sir."

Him, "When you can stop laughing
you can have your job back."

I haven't stopped laughing.

That job had a lot of responsibility I
didn't need. I'd rather just be Mail PO.
Get the same thing on my uniform.

Love, Mickey

P.S. Tell Don I tried to qualify for a golf
tournament and shot a clutch 89.

Phil

Dear Cheryl,

Is *Ozzie and Harriet* still on TV?
I used to think that show was corny as hell.
Now I dream of being married
with a buttload of kids.

I'd be pretty strict.
But no spankings.
I'd never hurt a kid.
Not even here.
I don't care if orders came from
General Westmoreland.

I carry memories of Nancy,
praying she's still waiting for me
in that other world where she sleeps
on clean sheets and a feather pillow.

We're going out on operations tomorrow, so
I thought someone should know there's a few
feelings under these filthy fatigues.

Love, Phil

P.S. This goddamned country rains horse piss—
      just emptied out my boots again—in case
      you meet a POG who wants to trade places.

Thanksgiving

Commander's Message

"This Thanksgiving Day we find ourselves in a foreign land assisting in the defense of the rights of free men everywhere. On this day we should offer our grateful thanks for the abundant life which we and our loved ones have been provided. May we each pray for His continued blessings and guidance upon our endeavors to assist the Vietnamese people in their struggle to attain an everlasting peace within a free society."

—W. C. Westmoreland, General
United States Army

Thanksgiving Menu

Shrimp Cocktail
Crackers

Roast Turkey	Cornbread Dressing
Giblet Gravy	Cranberry Sauce
Mashed Potatoes	Candied Sweet Potatoes

Buttered Peas

Assorted Crisp Relishes
Hot Butter Buns
Butter

Fruitcake
Mincemeat Pie
Pumpkin Pie with Whipped Cream

Assorted Fresh Fruit
Assorted Nuts
Assorted Candy
Tea   Milk   Coffee

Phil

Dear Cheryl,

My sister sent a present with her
last letter, a stuffed duck.
We named him Daffy—
he's our "unofficial mascot."

You otta see these
salt-dripping haggard rag-tags
having conversations with Daffy.
He wears a helmet (crushed beer can)
and jungle fatigues (woven razor grass).

Cap'n donated a soggy cigar.

Love ya, Phil

P.S. We're having Spam for Thanksgiving,
probably left over from WWI.

Alice's Restaurant

1964 Alice and Ray Brock purchase a gothic
revival building in Great Barrington, Massachusetts.
The small, pine church is transformed into a refuge,
where young people escape *establishment pressures*
and the hell of Vietnam.

Agitated neighbors shout at the long-haired,
nonconformists living in this *beatnik commune.*

Thanksgiving 1965 Arlo Guthrie, son of folk singer
Woody Guthrie, and a friend haul garbage from the
Brock's home to the city dump. Discovering it closed
for Thanksgiving, they toss the trash down a hill.

The pair is arrested, appearing before a blind judge,
who's unable to see the 8 x 10 glossy photos in evidence.
They plead guilty, pay a $25 fine, and clean up the mess.

"Alice's Restaurant Massacree" evolves into a satirical
18-minute talk-song that records the events. Later,
lyrics critical of the war are woven in.

Who says you can get anything you want?

Nancy

Tonight our professor is lecturing about navigating
life through *enlightenment*, explaining it's possible
to be *en-lightened* without reading a tome or spending
a hundred years in a monastery.

He says that according to existentialists,
most problems stem from *worrying* about
the past and future.

I worried, still worry, about Phil—Maybe
I never loved him as much as he loved me.
Otherwise why did I stop writing?

Now I worry that my feelings were *parataxic distortion*—
meaning, not based on Phil's true attributes,
but on a fantasy boyfriend I conjured in my mind.

I stay after class to talk to the professor about it.
He says, "Never let *learning* get in the way of *loving*."

Da Nang Vietnam

Inbound provisions:
Hot ammunition, maybe
even misplaced mail?

Phil

Cheryl,

A grunt just walked by.

KILL THEM ALL,
LET GOD SORT IT OUT!

scrawled on his flak jacket.

Put my dog tags in a boot.
If I hit a mine or a tripwire
that's all that'll be left.

Love, Phil

P.S. Forgot to explain POGs:
People Other than Grunts.
P.P.S. Just finished *The Carpetbaggers*.
First classic I ever read.

Cheryl

mom elopes with nuts & chews,
a drive-up ceremony in las vegas

since he owns a grocery store
we move to a new house with
tv dinners stacked in the freezer

salisbury steak is my favorite

mom and I used to get our periods
together.

now we're a week apart

Ziggy

My motel sign:

VACANCY

Chu Lai Vietnam

Gooks dig holes.
Two-feet deep.
Shove in Punji sticks—
18 inches of bamboo,
ends hacked to a point,
dipped in shit.

Stuck in holes,
camouflaged.
Neat little booby trap—
not the C-cup type.

Fuckin' crazy.

Medical Evacuation

From the standpoint of methods in which
soldiers are wounded—mines, high-velocity
missiles, booby-traps—and the locale of the
injured—paddy fields and along waterways
where human and animal excretion is common—

Vietnam is a dirty war

Due to the lack of secure road networks in
combat areas, med-evac choppers are keystone.

Whole blood packaged in Styrofoam™ containers
permits storage of 48–72 hours in the field,
in anticipation of casualties.

Greater care of the wounded results from rapid
evacuation, ready availability of whole blood,
well-established hospitals, and advanced surgical
techniques.

Mickey

USS *Hermitage LSD-34* Non-Virgin Islands

Dear Cheryl,

I can't believe you broke up with Don!

I'm still going out with that Chinese girl.
Her father works her to death,
I swear, 13 hours a day, 7 days a week.
They own a Chinese restaurant.

I sort of feel sorry for them because
they don't get hardly any business.
Her name is Yen, I'm serious.
She's from Hong Kong.

She's not exactly a girlfriend because
she's married and all.
Her husband is in Vietnam.

Love, Mickey

P.S. Tell Ziggy I won't be in the States for a while,
so she can stay stoned a little longer.

Ziggy

I sneak in the side door of the gas station,
drop a quarter in the cigarette machine,

and wonder if I have the strength
to push the right button,
straighten out my life.

Mick says I'm a nymphomaniac
when I'm really just in love.

Before I quit school, I told Ms. Hawes
that I moved in with my brother, and

she took me to the teacher's lounge,
poured two cups of coffee, gave me a
dime and the number of a church
where I could get help.

I spent it on a glazed donut.

Phil

Dear Cheryl,

We started packing maxi pads
in our helmets to plug sucking
chest wounds.

Another thing—
war flicks don't know shit about dying.
No one staggers in slow motion crying,
"Mama!"

They drop like puppets with
their strings cut.
Zapped.
Offed.
Lit up.
Dead as fucking door knobs.

I never prayed before I came here.

Love, Phil

P.S. My M-16's chipped, cracked,
metal parts worn through the bluing,
cuz it never leaves my side.
P.P.S. .45 is rusted shut.
Yo-yo can still walk-the-dog though.

Don

Dearest Cheryl,

DON'T TEAR THIS UP!!! PLEASE!!!

I'll do anything if you'll just forgive me.
Anything. I'm on my knees, begging, *please,*
I love you so much I can't eat or sleep.
All I think about is holding you.

I look for you everyday before and after school,
between classes, during nutrition at lunch.
Guess you've been cutting Hawes's class,
and using someone else's locker.
Has your mom told you I called?
About a million times!

PLEASE CALL ME!!!

I love you more today than ever, Don

P.S. Are you still pen pals with Mick & Phil?
P.P.S. I got that job at the club. $1.25 an hour.

Cheryl

Love is like sticking
your car keys in a pocket with
your sunglasses and thinking
your glasses won't get scratched.

Phil

2 a.m. December 1

Me and Gunther have guard duty in the
tower, a mini-hooch without the screen.

A 20-foot high platform,
Permanent Target Duty.

Thunk! Thunk! Thunk!

Mortars propel from some gook hooch.
I've got my buddy Blooper, an M-79 grenade launcher,
like a large bore, single barrel, sawn-off shotgun.

Our Xmas toys light up everything, moving or not.
M-18 Claymore mines—*front toward enemy*—
steel ball bearing shrapnel. Fugas. Trip flares.
Illumination flares, mini-chutes raining light.
Tracer rounds, ribbons of chrome-orange metal.

Hueys roll in.
Fighter pilots in helmets, shorts, zoris.
Annihilate the place. *Rat-a-tat-tat.*

Chaos.
Silent night, holy night.
Destruction.
All is calm, all is bright.
Extermination.
Sleep in heavenly peace.

Bits of beauty everywhere.

Cheryl

Stable horses, $2.50 an hour.

I broke all the rules, galloped
soon as I left the barn,

like dancing to "Hang on Sloopy,"
naked,

free.

Ziggy

Bubba dropped me at Hughes Market
with a list:

Crispy Critters
Ding Dongs
Potato Crisps
Sweet Tarts
Dr. Pepper

Wheeling through produce, I see
Cheryl's mom thumping cantaloupes.
Her cart cradles chickens, carrots, squash—
nothing in a can or a box.

"Ziggy!" she says, rushing over.
"Where've you been?"

I self-destruct on the spot.

Phil

I keep having this dream.
A short, sharp sound.

Click!

When I turn, a squat brown boy
jabs a gun in my gut.

Click! Click!

He swings the butt at my head.
I empty a clip in his face.

Bones fly. Chip by chip.
A tooth.

Another round of shoot-a-gook.

I wake up sweatin' blood.

God forgive us.

Mickey

USS *Hermitage LSD-34* Somewhere Over the Rainbow

Dear Cheryl,

What's the haps?

Thought I'd send you some stuff
I picked up on my travels.
Hope you like the poem about Santa Claus.

Guess what? I qualified for Heads Helmsman.
(That's the guy who steers the ship.)

Whenever we go through shallow water
I'll be called up to steer.
I have to know everything about the Pilot House.
If I make one mistake
I could run aground or into another ship.

I can't believe they'd give me so much
responsibility.

Later, Mickey

P.S. Last night I stepped into a card game
and walked out with $54.

Cheryl

Yesterday, I showed my mom the short story
I wrote as a makeup for Ms. Hawes's class
about a girl who stops taking crap from guys.

I got a dollar for my A.

This morning, Nuts & Chews set a gold
foil box on my place mat. Neatly folded
inside, an olive-green mohair sweater.
Cardigan, my size.

I think Mom's and my story will
have a happy ending, after all.

His name is Lou.

Ziggy

Imagine a family that chops, cooks,
eats their meals together?

Maybe I'll bake a cake today.

Angel or Devil's food?

Phil

Dear Cheryl,

Mama mined it.

Wrapped a bomb and
a baby in a blanket.
Blew two grunts to
smither-fuckin'-eens.

Whoever heard of a baby booby-trap?

Capt'n says we're fighting Commies
so our sons and daughters can crap
in a flush toilet.

All I want to do is come home in one piece
and make babies and live a quiet life in a
time and place without war.

With love, Phil

P.S. I hope I never get used to this.

Cheryl

It's unreal, like a movie, or photos in the newspaper, or Hollywood
actors, although I know that's not true, not really, but it's easier, safer,
to think of them as fake soldiers touched up with makeup, red-dye
blood, it *is* easier, *was* easier, to pretend the war is a movie, but I know
it's real, because Phil's real, and his letters are real, and now I wish I'd
been paying more attention to all the Gunthers and Phils on the news,
and I've decided to spend six months allowance on books of tickets for
Disneyland and I'm going to tear out all the "E" tickets for Phil. . . .

Phu Bai Vietnam

Cold C-ration breakfast.
Pack up.
Move out.

Cold C-ration lunch,
ham and lima beans,
warmed on an exhaust
manifold.

March.

Frag grenades.
Body count.

Another crappy meal.

Mickey

USS *Hermitage LSD-34* DEEP SHIT

Dear Cheryl,

I'm up to my ass now.

First, on the way back from Bermuda
I got caught sleeping on watch. Second,
I got in a fight in the chow line and was taken
straight to the Executive Officer's stateroom.

He said, "This is it sailor. No more chances."

Then I got busted drinking on a phony ID
and spent the night in jail. The next morning
I was right back up here.

Guess I won't get liberty for a while.

Love, Mickey

P.S. My new girlfriend says I'm a godless alcoholic.
That slays me!

Ziggy

cheryl,

this is the last page in my journal and i wanted to tell you that i don't know why i did it—it wasn't about mickey or don or me—mostly it wasn't about me because i'm nothing and that proves it because only a nothing would do what i did in the gas station and then something like that to her best friend—and i don't expect you or god to forgive me because i'll never forgive myself—but i saw your mom at the store and she looked so happy and i know it's because she's in love and married a nice man and i think it's about time someone in our crowd was happy and i'm extra glad it's you.

me

Phil

Darvon Date.

White powder buffers a tiny pink pill
inside a red and white capsule. The infirmary
prescribes them instead of aspirin.

Supposed to be better for our guts, since
we drink like fish and eat street crap.

I split the hulls,
stash the pills,
trash the rest.

Pretty and pink, she sinks into a
red, white, and blue-edged envelope.
I free her with my tongue, chase her
down with warm beer.

A perfect girlfriend who knows how
to take my mind off everything that's
happening here.

Nancy

Professor James is wearing a Betty Crocker
apron, brandishing a broom, lecturing on the
general unhappiness of women in our society.

He says television and movies, newspapers
and magazines, schools and even our
parents are manipulating us into thinking

housewife is synonymous with *occupation*.

He says women are victims of a false belief
system that expects us to find meaning in our
lives through our husbands and raising children.

"Housework can be done by any 8-year-old,"
he says, trading the broom for a paperback,
The Feminine Mystique by Betty Friedan.

"Who would like to borrow it?"

I raise my hand.

Cheryl

Phil's in Nam.
Not Nancy.
Not Ziggy.
Not me.

Why? Anatomy?
Ejaculator versus baby maker?
Does that make him expendable?

Who hasn't said,

I wish he was dead.
I'm mad enough to kill.
If words were bullets
    he'd be pushing up daisies.

I scream that and more about
The-Dirty-Rotten-Two-Timer.

Bang. Bang. He's history.

If thoughts are things
a murderer resides in my head.

Ziggy

Bubba's still asleep so I fire up a
breakfast doobie and polish off a
package of Lorna Doone cookies.

I find Ms. Hawes in the phone book
and call to tell her I'm still writing in
my journal and ask if it's okay to send
her a poem sometime, but I'd understand

if it's not, because she has over 250 students
a day if you count all of her English classes,
plus homeroom and after school detention
and,

she asks if I can help her out on Sunday.
I'm too stoned to come up with an excuse.

Now what?

Phil

Gunther.

Something gets his arm at the elbow,
and he gives a funny little wave, like
a flag salute, watching his hand crawl
on the ground.

Head down, he mutters, "Crap-ola,"
as if he'd dropped his only glove.
Then he passes out, real laid-back.

Medic.
Tourniquet.
Whole blood.
Morphine.

I hold him, my fingers clenched into fists.
He squeezes back, still alive, hanging on.
Jesus, there's too much blood.

Cheryl

Phil wrote about Gunther getting wounded, said it was nothing serious, that Gunther was one lucky son-of-a-bitch with his million-dollar injury, because the war was over for him and he'd be back in the world soon, but I wish he'd told me what happened, because my whole body shakes when I think about him getting hurt, because I know Gunther, even though I've never met him, I picture this big, sweet guy in a Santa suit (so his buddies can have a laugh in hell) wearing his girlfriend's garter belt (because he misses her so much) and I think about Pastor Brunner playing his guitar in Sunday school and how I used to think God was a musician and I was one of his instruments, and believing he was strumming me, keeping me safe for eternal life, and I can't believe anyone could be so brainwashed, even a five-year-old kid, and before I know it I'm playing "Nowhere Man" on Mickey's guitar. . . .

Mickey

USS Hermitage LSD-34

From: SECNAV P. H. Nitze

To: All Ships and Stations

Subject: WAVES (**W**omen **A**ccepted for **V**olunteer **E**mergency **S**ervice)

1. The following information will be of utmost interest to all sailors ashore and afloat.

2. After a lengthy effort the WAVES began service in August 1942, thus avoiding a crisis at hand. Each vessel averages 125 lbs., 66 in. length, and is broad across the beam with dual forward mounts. Newer models are best launched at night, free and fast as hell.

3. A creative, yet functional design supports a hatch at mid-ship that accepts a driving shaft between 6 and 8 inches, though her engine must be heated to the optimum temperature. If bearings are well lubricated the standard speed is 60 minutes, 15 minutes if full speed ahead.

4. If operated according to the manual she will shudder and shake when backing off an all-out run, no matter who's at the helm. Do not disclose secret maneuvers except in the line of duty. It is mandatory to report violations.

5. Will raise an OFF LIMITS flag 3 to 7 days each month to unload disposable hazardous waste and repair damage caused by projectiles with loose screws. Reel in hoses and salute her colors to avoid a hostile disposition. Hull seldom needs scraping or paint, though perfume is appreciated.

6. With proper care these vessels will operate satisfactorily until every sailor receives his discharge orders.

"The Unknown Chaplain"

Dust-Off

"Voodoo 10! Voodoo 10!
This is Orphan 99.
Request urgent dust-off.
U.S. Marine . . .
mine . . . mine."

"99, this is 10.
Extent of injuries?
Is landing zone secure?"

"Urgent!
Repeat . . . gent!
Marine bleed . . .
Chri . . . mighty . . .
get that damn bird. . . ."

"You're OK soldier.
Say again, 99.
Slowly."

"10, this is 99.
LZ secure . . .
. . . no enemy fire.
Need . . ."

"Roger that.
Choppers airborne.
What's your position?"

"Zebra 109-271 . . .
Repeat, Zebra 109-271."

Dust-off complete:
19 minutes.

Marine dies over rice paddy.

Ziggy

Outside L.A. Mission:

Old men sleep on sidewalks.
Cardboard mattresses.
Pockets inside out.
Stolen shoes.

Ms. Hawes says,
"Don't be afraid."

I'm not.

Phil

Cheryl,

All I've done for the last 42 hours
is wade through muck and mud.
Every inch of exposed flesh
is sliced up from busting jungle.
The fever blisters on my lips are
scabbed over with rot.

Tomorrow we're going on a seek-and-destroy
patrol. We don't like these skinny Commies
using us for target practice.

If we have to, we'll take the village apart one
straw at a time. Shoot a few dogs and chickens,
maybe a water buffalo.

Right now my cartridge belt has
1 Bowie knife + 180 rounds of ammo on it.
I have a rifle that shoots 20 rounds
in less than 2 seconds
plus 6 grenades.
Fragmentation type. 14 ounces.

I pity the poor gook that crosses my path.
I want to get at least one for Gunther.

Thou shalt not kill—Fuck that shit!

I want to come home, Phil

Cheryl

I can't get out of bed, strangling in sheets, soaked with tears, drool, snot—screaming louder than when Daddy died and I wore white gloves and a black headband like Caroline Kennedy at her dad's funeral—I'm crying for Daddy and Gunther, and I can't even imagine how Phil feels—and I'm tearing at my pillow until my fingers are raw and I'm numb inside trying to understand, *How can someone fucking bleed to death in nineteen minutes?*

Mickey

USS *Hermitage LSD-34* Pussy Patrol

Don—

Check it out: More than 1,000 sailors
lined-up on deck with our flies open
and our dicks hanging out.

Master Sergeant says, "What's the gag?"

We salute, all serious.
"If we're gonna work like horses
we're gonna look like horses, *Sir!*"

"The Mick"

P.S. Man, I've been off my game.
Can't sink a stinkin' bar of soap
in the drain with the butt of my rifle.
P.P.S. I hear you got that job.
Better let your peeps play free!

Ziggy

Ms. Hawes shows me around the Mission,
where women stay up all night taking turns
at an ironing board, pressing work clothes
for the next day.

An older lady reminds me of Nana,
rhinestone clips in her silver hair.
She got laid off from J.C. Penny,
then evicted from her apartment.

"A neighbor brought me here," she says,
but not like she's feeling sorry for herself.
"Tomorrow I'll look for a another job."

She smiles and pats the blanket on her cot.
I settle on the edge. She smells like Ivory Snow.
She shows me pictures of her kids, grandkids,
too ashamed to tell them what happened.

"I'll wait until I get back on my feet,"
she says.

Nancy

I told my parents I'm spending the night at Cheryl's house,
but I'm really taking a bus to Berkeley with my Psych class
to join thousands of protesters. A 10-hour ride.

My suitcase is filled with rag dolls I made out of socks
in red, white, and blue. Uncle Sam hats cut from cardboard.

I want you!

Professor James says he'll dress up like a soldier in the
American Revolutionary War. We'll march behind coffins
filled with copies of the Declaration of Independence.

Life, Liberty, and the pursuit of Happiness

I'll burn my rag dolls, standing with draftees burning
induction orders and draft cards.

Hell no! We won't go!
No one knows what we're fighting for!
Hell no!

Cheryl

Hi Ziggy,

I got your letter and I can't believe I'm writing back, but so much bad stuff has happened, and our country is in such a mess, but mostly I can't stand the thought of losing you, and I miss you and everything about you, even puking in my popcorn. Ha! Ha! I don't blame you the same way I blame Don because I know you were stoned out of your mind and crazy nuts after losing the baby, but I don't understand why Don did it? Not if he really loved me, like he kept saying. Now I know he never did. Not *really*. And I'll never forgive him. *Never.* But you're still my best friend, and I had to tell you before someone drops a bomb on us. Girls rock! Girls rule!

Love, Cheryl

Phil

Pages of the new testament fill my pillow,
gospels on a recon in search of a soul.

Mickey

USS *Hermitage LSD-34* World Traveler

Dear Cheryl,

Look at all the places I've been
since hooking up with the Navy:

Boston
Miami
Virginia
New York
Washington, DC
Halifax
Cuba
Jamaica
Puerto Rico
Virgin Islands

I'll double that next year when we make
a Mediterranean cruise—Unless we go to
Vietnam which is a definite possibility.

Love, "The Mick"

Ziggy

Fat tits + quick wit

does not = stupidity

if that's what you think.

Phil

Dear Cheryl,

Sarge just strolled in.
Told me to get my shit together.
A truck's leaving for the airport in Pleiku in 30 minutes.
He snatched my M-16 and walked out,
not another word.

Fuck it! I'm gone! I'm coming home, baby!

Love ya, Phil

Cheryl

I'm wiggin' out over *Dr. Kildare*, that dimple
in his chin and those dreamy blue eyes, humming
the theme song "Three Stars Will Shine Tonight."

Ziggy storms in like the good old days,
hair in soup can rollers,

"Bob Dylan crashed his motorcycle.
Broken neck.
Concussion.
Critical condition."

We sob listening to his album *Highway 61 Revisited*,
singing "It Takes a Lot to Laugh, It Takes a Train to Cry."

I unpin her rollers, brush out her hair.
She irons mine. "Let's go cruisin'."

We drag Van Nuys Boulevard in Bubba's beater,
flirting with bleached blond surfers in a woodie.

Ziggy peels out, ditching them for Bob's Big Boy,
cranking The Lovin' Spoonful, "Do You Believe in Magic?"

We share a banana split, extra whip cream and cherries,
celebrating 2 hours, 43 minutes without talking about the
two you-know-whos.

"Who needs them?"

It's 1966

and
> Valley of the Dolls *by Jacqueline Susann*
> *breaks bookselling records*

and
> *Johnson says, "To know war*
> *is to know that there is still*
> *madness in this world"*

and
> *the Beatles top the charts,*
> "We Can Work It Out"

and
> *American troops in Vietnam*
> *double in size to 400,000*

and
> *correspondent Bill Rowley*
> *travels with a patrol in Vietnam*
> *giving a vivid account, "GIs holding the*
> *rifles above their heads . . . one just fell."*

and
> *80,000 Americans are killed*
> *or wounded in Vietnam*

and
> *the president's daughter,*
> *Luci Baines Johnson, gets married*
> *with a 13-tier 300-pound cake*
> *decorated with swans*

and
> Captain Kangaroo *is the only*
> *live-action show on TV.*

1965 Timeline

January 2. The Selma Voting Rights Movement officially begins when Dr. Martin Luther King, Jr. speaks at a meeting in Brown Chapel, which becomes the starting point for the Selma to Montgomery marches in 1965. The gathering is in direct defiance of an anti-meeting ordinance.

January 20. Lyndon B. Johnson is sworn in as President of the United States. He remarks, "We can never again stand aside, prideful in isolation. Terrific dangers and troubles that we once called 'foreign' now constantly live among us."

January 27. National Security Advisor McGeorge Bundy and Defense Secretary Robert McNamara send a memo to President Johnson declaring that America's limited military engagement in Vietnam is not succeeding, stating that the U.S. stands at a "fork in the road" and must either escalate its involvement or withdraw.

February 18. Jimmie Lee Jackson walks with other African Americans in Marion, Alabama to protest obstructions in voter registration. Local police and Alabama State Troopers forcefully break up the unarmed protesters using bull-whips, billy clubs, and tear gas. Jackson and his sister, mother, and 82-year old grandfather seek refuge inside a café. Jackson is shot in the stomach by an Alabama State Trooper, chased into the street, and brutally beaten.

February 21. Malcolm X is assassinated at a speaking engagement at the Audubon Ballroom in New York. Three gunmen charge the stage, shooting him 15 times at close range. The 39-year-old minister and political rights activist is pronounced dead at New York's Presbyterian Hospital.

February 21. Augustus Owsley Stanley III operates a makeshift laboratory in the bathroom of a house near the University of California, Berkeley. The lab is raided by police who are searching for methamphetamine. They only find LSD, which was not illegal at the time.

February 26. 27-year-old Jimmie Lee Jackson dies at Good Samaritan Hospital in Selma from an infection associated with his gunshot wound.

February 27. Malcolm X's funeral is held at the Faith Temple Church of God in Harlem with 1,500 people in attendance. After the ceremony, friends pick up the gravediggers' shovels and bury their leader themselves.

March 7. Between 500 and 600 civil rights activists march east from Selma, Alabama. After crossing Edmund Pettus Bridge, they encounter state troopers and are ordered to disband. Soon thereafter, unprovoked troopers begin shoving demonstrators, knocking them down and beating them with nightsticks. Another detachment begins hurling tear gas. Images of bloodied and severely injured protesters flash across news media evoking the name "Bloody Sunday."

March 8. Da Nang, Vietnam. 3,500 U.S. Marines land at China Beach to defend the American air base. They join 23,000 U.S. military advisors already stationed in the country.

March 9. Two days after Bloody Sunday, Dr. King leads 2,500 people in a symbolic march to Edmund Pettus Bridge in Selma. They kneel for a prayer session and sing hymns. Afterward, they march back, thereby obeying a court order against marching all the way to Montgomery.

March 9. Selma, Alabama. Three white ministers are attacked and beaten with clubs outside a café where segregationist whites are known to gather. One victim, James Reeb, a Unitarian Universalist minister from Boston, is rushed to Selma's public hospital where he is refused treatment.

March 9. President Johnson sanctions Napalm-B for use in Vietnam. When dropped from "hedgehoppers"—planes flying around 100 feet—the antipersonnel bomb showers a surface area with flames about 270 feet long and 75 feet wide.

March 11. Minister Reeb dies at University Hospital in Birmingham with his wife by his side.

March 16. Federal District Court Judge Frank M. Johnson, Jr. rules in favor of civil rights activists wishing to march peacefully from Selma to Montgomery, Alabama. He cites, "The law is clear that the right to petition one's government for the redress of grievances may be exercised in large groups . . . These rights may . . . be exercised by marching, even along public highways." (Williams v. Wallace, 1960)

March 21–25. Dr. King leads 3,200 protesters in a march from Selma to Montgomery, walking approximately 12 miles per day and sleeping in fields. The Southern Christian Leadership Conference (SCLC) and the Student Nonviolent Coordinating Committee (SNCC) arranges logistics—providing food, water, and sanitation. Dr. King delivers his "How Long, Not Long" speech on the steps of the Alabama State Capitol in Montgomery.

April 1. President Johnson sanctions additional Marine battalions and up to 20,000 logistical personnel in Vietnam. American combat troops are authorized to patrol rural areas and flush out Viet Cong. The decision to permit offensive operations is kept secret from the American public for two months.

April 15. U.S. and South Vietnamese fighter-bombers drop a thousand tons of bombs on Viet Cong positions.

April 17. Students for a Democratic Society (SDS) organize the first national march to protest the Vietnam War. More than 20,000 people assemble, a turnout that surprises the organizers. SDS President Paul Potters speaks to demonstrators in front of the Washington Monument.

April 20. General Westmoreland meets with other top aides. They agree to recommend to the president that he send another 40,000 combat soldiers to Vietnam.

May 13. The United States enacts the first halt in bombings in hopes that Hanoi will negotiate. There are six additional bombing pauses in the Rolling Thunder campaign, all with the same goal. The North Vietnamese ignore the peace offerings, using the respite to restore air defenses and dispatch troops and supplies to the South by way of the Ho Chi Minh trail.

May 19. The United States resumes bombing of North Vietnam.

July 28. President Johnson announces he will send another 44 combat battalions to Vietnam, raising the U.S. military presence to 125,000. Monthly draft call will double to 35,000. "I have asked the commanding general, General Westmoreland, what more he needs to meet this mounting aggression. He has told me. And we will meet his needs. We cannot be defeated by force of arms. We will stand in Vietnam."

August 6. President Johnson signs the Voting Rights Act, which follows the language of the 15th Amendment. Literacy tests, poll taxes, and other requirements that were used to restrict black voting are made illegal. Other provisions include special enforcement terms directed at those parts of the country where Congress believes the potential for discrimination is the greatest.

August 11–16. The arrest of Marquette Frye, a 21-year-old black man, sparks 5 days of riots in Watts, a neighborhood in South Los Angeles. During the course of the riots, there are 34 deaths and 1,032 reported injuries. The estimated loss of property exceeds $40 million, mostly due to damage by fire. The Watts Riots are the worst of a series of disturbances that break out across the country during the summer of 1965.

August 12. The Vietnam Day Committee (VDC), a powerful force in antiwar activities, stages a demonstration designed to disrupt trains with soldiers embarking to Vietnam via the Oakland Army Terminal.

August 30. President Johnson signs a bill that adds four words to the Selective Service law, "knowingly destroys, knowingly mutilates." This refers to draft registration and classification cards held by men in the United States between the ages of 18 and 35.

September 24. President Johnson issues Executive Order 11246 to enforce affirmative action, stating that civil rights laws alone are not enough to rectify discrimination. It obligates government contractors to "take affirmative action" toward prospective minority employees in all areas of hiring and employment.

October 15–16. Antiwar rallies draw as many as 100,000 in 80 major U.S. cities, as well as globally in London, Paris, and Rome.

October 18. David Miller becomes the first activist arrested under the new Selective Service law for knowingly destroying his draft card.

October 30. Five Medal of Honor recipients lead a march of 25,000 people in support of the U.S. involvement in Vietnam.

November 14–16. The Battle of la Drang Valley is the first major battle between U.S. troops and North Vietnamese Army regulars (NVA) within the bounds of South Vietnam. Seventy-nine Americans are killed and 121 are wounded. NVA losses are approximately 2,000.

November 30. Upon his return from a visit to Vietnam, Defense Secretary McNamara warns that the American casualty rate may be up to 1,000 dead per month.

By the end of 1965, U.S. troop levels reach 184,300. It is estimated that 90,000 South Vietnamese soldiers have deserted, and 35,000 soldiers from North Vietnam have infiltrated the South. Up to 50 percent of the countryside in South Vietnam is under some measure of control by the Viet Cong.

During the entire war, the United States will fly 3 million missions and drop approximately 8 million tons of bombs, which represents four times the amount of tonnage dropped during World War II and the largest display of firepower in the history of warfare.

General Willliam C. Westmoreland is chosen by *Time* magazine as 1965's "Man of the Year."

Acknowledgments

First, this book would not have been remotely possible if it weren't for my small, but intimate circle of friends in high school, especially my first serious boyfriend. (You know who you are.) Unbelievable, that I kept dozens of their letters, stored in a shoebox for more than forty years.

Second, I applaud the faculty in the MFA program in Writing for Children and Young Adults at Vermont College of Fine Arts for encouraging us all to push the creative envelope, especially my faculty advisors Ron Koertge and Tim Wynne-Jones. I remain grateful for the undeniable friendship of "The Unreliable Narrators."

Third, I am beyond fortunate to have Kelli Chipponeri and Greg Jones as my editors at Running Press Kids and Jill Corcoran as my agent. All carry an extraordinary compassionate gene and are equally passionate about books for young people.

Fourth, I am grateful for my two writing families, Cambria Writers Workshop, and, most affectionately, Kiddie Writers, always willing to wring out a hanky over rejections and eager to pop a cork over successes.

Fifth, I treasure my mom (who survived my teen years, barely), Lou (for sharing his crazy Navy stories), daughter Krise (who makes me laugh when I need it most), daughter Kyle (who reads to our boys every single night), Jon (who puts up with us), and grandsons Michael (who thinks I'm famous), Cooper (who never rats me out), and Chase (who shares his finger food).

Sixth, I am indebted to my partner and best friend on the entire planet, Phillip Cole, not only because he was essential to the writing and revision of this story, but for a gazillion other nameless reasons.

Seventh, my utmost admiration for the two-and-a-half million American soldiers who braved the living hell of Vietnam from March 8, 1965 when the first combat troops landed at China Beach to the fall of Saigon on April 30, 1975.

An Intimate Conversation with
Sherry Shahan, author of *Purple Daze*

Q: *Purple Daze* is a story about love, friendship, and rock 'n' roll. It plays out on a stage shared by riots, assassinations, and war. Why did you decide to focus on this particular period?

A: While cleaning out my office closet, I found a tattered shoebox filled with letters written by a friend who was in Vietnam in the 1960s. I spent hours pouring through gut-wrenching accounts of his day-to-day life in that living hell.

It was heartbreaking to watch a close friend turn from a carefree guy who just wanted to hang out with his friends into a hardened soldier. I knew I had to do something with his letters; after all, I'd kept them all this time.

The more I researched the 1960s, the more I realized I needed to narrow the book's timeline. I chose 1965, in part because of the Watts Riots in Los Angeles. By the time it ended, 34 people had been killed, another 1,032 injured, and 3,438 were arrested. Nearly 1,000 buildings were damaged or destroyed.

Q: The characters in your story are faced with difficult issues: abortion, drugs, and war. Did writing the story using an unconventional form help you tackle these issues?

A: After reading my friend's letters, I started messing around with other writing styles. Journals, notes, poems. I wrote character sketches about my crazy friends in high school. Once I began scribbling, it was a constant flashback. Memories assaulted me twenty-four-seven. *Bam, bam, bam.*

I knew I wanted to be inside the head of each character to explore his or her innermost thoughts and feelings, not just describe the character from the outside looking in. I could have done this with an omniscient viewpoint—but bouncing in and out of several minds could confuse readers. Instead, I chose journal entries, letters, free verse, and traditional poetry.

Q: What stumbling blocks did you encounter writing a novel in verse?

A: What began as a stream of consciousness had to be shaped into a story with a compelling beginning, middle, and end. Each character demanded his or her own story arc. Yet each story had to be woven seamlessly into the whole. Talk about a challenge!

I became obsessed with metaphor, assonance, startling imagery, rhythm, and cadence. Even white space—meaning the negative space on a page—played a role in shaping my characters' emotions. Example:

Ziggy

Fat tits + quick wit

does not = stupidity

if that's what you think.

Phil

Pages of the new testament fill my pillow,

gospels on a recon in search of a soul.

These two poems are short—yet I think they say volumes about the characters even more than if I'd filled a page with margin-to-margin prose.

To me, verse mirrors the pulse of adolescent life. Condensed metaphoric language on a single page is a good reflection of their tightly packed world. Emotions are where teens live.

Q: How did you go about researching *Purple Daze*? Was your approach different from your other work?

A: Because *Purple Daze* is set in a real time and place, I read countless accounts of the 1960s, including *The Things They Carried* by Tim O'Brien. I talked to dozens of Vietnam vets. One guy told me he put a condom over the muzzle of his rifle to help keep out steel-rusting moisture, yet he could shoot through it. Another guy told me it was common to remove tobacco from packs of cigarettes and replace it with marijuana.

During that same time, one of my friends had enlisted in the Navy. He spent his days cruising the Caribbean, getting drunk, and chasing women. Such vastly different experiences expressed the utter craziness of the times. I knew these details would go in the book too.

Q: Amidst the poetry you have inserted certain—for lack of a better term—*news reports* about what was going on in the world, e.g., assassinations, riots, etc. With so many events to pick from, how did you select what would go in the book?

A: When I read about Norman Morrison, father of three, who set himself on fire to protest the war, I sat at my computer crying. His piece was included late in the copyedit stage.

Norman Morrison
(December 29, 1933–November 2, 1965)

A devout Quaker and father of three young children pours kerosene over his head and sets himself on fire outside Secretary of Defense Robert McNamara's office at the Pentagon in an act of self-sacrifice to protest United States involvement in the Vietnam War.

The narrative pieces were chosen because I thought they were fascinating or horrifying or both. I added the story behind Arlo Guthrie's famed song "Alice's Restaurant Massacree" as a lighthearted anecdote. I could have added more history, but I didn't want *Purple Daze* to be "textbook-ish."

Ultimately, it's a story about six friends and their sometimes humorous, often painful, and ultimately dramatic lives.

Q: You went to high school in Los Angeles in the 1960s, right?

A: Yeah, it was crazy in LA back then. One time, my friends and I snuck out in the middle of the night to check out the underworld of drunks and strip joints on Skid Row. During the Watts Riots, we drove the smoky freeways, looking for a break in the National Guard barrier. We were intent on seeing the fires and destruction up close. We were such adrenaline junkies!

Q: The book feels very intimate. It made me wonder, is the character Cheryl really you in disguise?

A: There are still small holes outside my bedroom door from a hook and eye. That was my mom's attempt to keep me from sneaking out at night. Like the character Cheryl, I simply crawled out the window.

In one scene, Cheryl and Ziggy are piercing each other's ears. They're using frozen potatoes to numb them, sort of like an earlobe sandwich. The Animals are wailing, "We Gotta Get out of This Place."

And, yep, just like Cheryl, I really did shave between my eyebrows.

Q: Nancy's behavior toward her boyfriend at the end of the novel was interesting. But you don't apologize for her or justify her distance from Phil. Can you talk about that a bit?

A: Like most circles of friends, mine was a jumble of diverse personalities. Nancy is based on one of them. She was much more mature than the rest of us. I guess it never occurred to me to try to justify her pulling away. To me, sending Phil a "Dear John" letter showed a thoughtful decision to take her life in a different direction—a direction that was precipitated by his being in Vietnam.

Q: What do you hope your readers will take away from *Purple Daze*?

A: While I never consciously write with the intent of slapping my readers over the head with a message, the difficulties facing today's teens aren't all that different from those teens faced in the sixties, like issues with parents, relationships, love, and loss.

Teenagers are still breaking away from authority and convention, still forging their way into an unknown future. And unfortunately, our country is still engaged in a war of choice on foreign soil.

Q: Tell us something no one knows about you.

A: Only if you promise not to tell! Shortly after "Phil" (real name, Bill) came home from Vietnam, we entered a dance contest at a local bar. What a dive! We got together a couple of times beforehand so I could practice turning under his lead. Guess what? We won!

Q: If you were to write a letter to yourself as a teen what would you say?

A: Something like this:

Dear Sheri,

Frizzy hair and freckles. Braces. Flat-chested. Nair slathered on your legs. Your mom wouldn't let you shave. You shaved between your eyebrows, because she wouldn't let you pluck. (Trust me, you could have sneaked the tweezers without her knowing.) Did you really put toilet paper in your bra? Uh, let's not go there. . . .

You always found a way to adapt to challenging situations. Since you could only go out on Friday nights, you crawled out of your bedroom window on Saturday nights. (You have to admit, Mom used a sense of humor when she tied a bell to the shade so she'd know when you came in.)

But . . . driving to downtown Los Angeles in the middle of the night to check out Skid Row? Cutting classes and forging your mom's name on medical excuses? That's crazy stuff!

Things usually started out innocently enough, like the time you "borrowed" a friend's car without permission. (He kept his keys in the ashtray, for chrissake!) Plowing into a parked car was an accident. The day went from bad to worse when the police showed up during high school. Grand Theft Auto. *Are you kidding me?* Reduced to Joy Riding. Okay, that's better. Still, you were on probation for six months.

You did some pretty stupid stuff during your tumultuous teen years. But that doesn't mean you *were* stupid. It's just that the manual for surviving high school hadn't been written. It still hasn't. (When is someone going to write the damn manual?) Seriously, though, I've always been one of your biggest fans. I'm proud to have been part of your life.

I'm particularly proud of you for writing to Bill the whole time he was in Vietnam. In fact, you kept writing long after others stopped, including his girlfriend. There were times when your letters were his only connection to a time and place without M16s and Napalm.

Guess what? Bill and your other close friends inspired *Purple Daze*—a young adult novel you wrote as an adult.

Do you remember this poem? Your scribbled it in ninth grade during a particularly depressing time:

> Graveyards and headstones
> are merely a lie.
> People never live
> therefore they can't die.

It's in the book too. You only had one boyfriend in high school. Let's call him Don, because that's his name. I used his real name in the novel. See? You grew up to be one brave woman!

A few things to remember:

1. People in positions of authority (parents, teachers, employers) aren't always right. Fire the doctor who said you couldn't get pregnant.
2. Don't worry about your frizzy hair. It goes stick straight in your first trimester.
3. It's okay not to tell your boyfriend all your secrets. But never hide the truth from yourself.
4. A skinned knee will heal.

Love,
Sherry

Tips and tricks for the verse writer

Over the years, Sherry Shahan has attended numerous poetry workshops, including intense studies in Paris and Istanbul. Although writing a story in verse isn't for everyone, she offers up tips for those interested in giving it a try.

Sherry believes novels in verse have the power to bring readers closer to the consciousness of their characters. Maybe even closer than novels written in traditional margin-to-margin prose. When should a writer consider this form?

1. Stories that are better told from more one than one character's point of view. Mel Glenn's verse novel *Who Killed Mr. Chippendale?* has more than fifty viewpoint characters. Even if Glenn had used an omniscient viewpoint—in other words, bouncing in and out of every character's mind—it could be confusing to the reader. However, not all verse novels have more than one viewpoint character.

2. Stories that are predominantly character driven, as opposed to action driven. Verse novels tend to deal with highly charged emotional issues. Some issues include: incest (*Because I Am Furniture* by Thalia Chaltas), mental illness (*Stop Pretending: What Happened When My Big Sister Went Crazy* by Sonya Sones), and teen pregnancy (*The First Part Last* by Angela Johnson). In each of these stories, what the characters are thinking and feeling is more important than what they're doing.

3. Stories with poetry as a subplot or theme. In *Locomotion*, Jacqueline Woodson's main character, Lonnie, is exploring poetic forms to help him deal with the untimely death of his parents. In Ron Koertge's *Shakespeare Bats Cleanup*, the main character is bedridden. He's a bored kid who reads his dad's poetry books and then begins writing his own poems.

4. Stories that are best told in short, energetic bursts—instead of traditional margin-to-margin prose. For example, scenes that capture one moment, whether it be an emotion or an idea.

5. Try this exercise: Choose a paragraph from one of your stories. Then throw out every rule about sentence structure and punctuation. Instead, concentrate on metaphor, assonance, imagery, rhythm, and pulse. Shouldn't all good writing contain these elements? Sure. But I find it easier to focus on "voice sounds" and "patterns of expression" when my writing *looks* like poetry.

Purple Daze Playlist

In the 1960s our cars were big and old and loud. Our radios were cranked to rock stations KFWB, KHJ, or KRLA in Los Angeles. Back then, I'd huddle under my covers at night, ear against my transistor radio, listening to inimitable DJ personalities, such as Huggy Boy, Dave Hull "the Hullabalooer," and Casey Kasem.

While writing *Purple Daze*, I blasted Aretha Franklin, Janis Joplin, Jimi Hendrix, the Beatles, the Rolling Stones, and Jefferson Airplane.

I think of the music of the 1960s as the decade of protest songs, voicing strong feelings about the Vietnam War. The songs were played during anti-war demonstrations and marches. Their lyrics still resonate today.

Here are the protest songs I remember most:

"Where Have All the Flowers Gone?", Pete Seeger (1961)
"The Times They Are a-Changin'", Bob Dylan (1964)
"Eve of Destruction", Barry McGuire and P.F. Sloan (1965)
"I Ain't Marching Anymore", Phil Ochs (1965)
"Universal Soldier", Donovan (1965)
"Alice's Restaurant Massacree", Arlo Guthrie (1967)
"I-Feel-Like-I'm-Fixin'-to-Die", Country Joe and the Fish (1967)
"Abraham, Martin and John", Dion (1968)
"Five to One", The Doors (1968)
"People Got to be Free", The Rascals (1968)
"Sky Pilot", Eric Burton and the Animals (1968)
'The Unknown Soldier", The Doors (1968)
"Fortunate Son", Creedence Clearwater Revival (1969)
"Gimme Shelter", The Rolling Stones (1969)
"Give Peace a Chance", John Lennon (1969)
"Wooden Ships", Crosby, Stills & Nash and Jefferson Airplane (1969)

Rock 'n' roll is here to stay!

Lance Corporal William
"Bill" Rose (left),
US Marines, Vietnam, 1966.

1st "Sher
Thes is my self
+ Butler top
of our g....... I am
holding the shells
for our 50 caliber
machine Gun +
Butler is gitting
set to chamber
a round. It
was taken oct & 66
at one of the few
time during this
month that it
wasn't raining
Bill

5,000-gallon jet fuel tanker with "lucky" bullet hole in door.
E-4 Phillip Manor, US Army, Vietnam, 1969.

The "real" Mickey below deck on the
USS Hermitage LSD-34, 1966.

Original letter written to Sherry by Bill
during his time in Vietnam, 1966.

Dearest Sheri   Sept 27, 1966

Well beautiful last night was the first of 9 for me on guard duty. I about froze my tail off. Between the wind & the rain & the fact that it is starting to get cold I wasen't at all sleeping during my whole watch. I was on 1 hrs & off for 2 hrs.

Right now It is 4:00 Tuesday afternoon. I tried to go to mass today but after I walked all the way to Fox Company the chaplin ddn't show up. I am back at my outpost & so is a damn near dead Vietnamese farmer. He stepped on a land mine near his house. He has quite a few holes in him & a lot of his intestines are exposed. The helicopters that are used for Evacuation are all out picking up dead & wounded grunts from a recon patrol that was ambused about 2 hrs ago.

It will take them another 45 minutes to get up here & by that time the coremen said he would be dead.

Life is cheap here I hope if I get shot the helicopter are near enough to pick me up.

It has been 14 days since I heard from my girl so the last few days I quit writting her.

I've been putting my thoughts to you. You may not be my girl but you care enough to answer my letter & let me know you appreciate hearing from me. Thats really nice of you.

Hows your beautiful dark stomach there. I'll bet it is going to start getting lighter pretty soon. although it rains over there almost always when it isn't the sun is shining & its making me look like a niger.

I dreampt last night (during the 4 hrs sleep I got) that I got shot four times in the gut. that dream was so damn real that when I woke up I was actually surprised I wasen't in a navy hospital.

Have I mentioned that I miss being home latly brother. I sure do. I am so bugged about no mail from you know who. That I half ways wish I would get shot up bad enough to be sent home.

But I wouldn't gain much by that because I would have a rough time getting up to your pad to sneak out with me certain that I know. YOU

Love Bill

~223~

Transcription of Bill's letter:

Sept 27, 1966

Dearest Sheri

Well beautiful, last night was the first of 7 for me on guard duty. I about froze my tail off. Between the wind the rain & the fact that it is starting to get cold I wasn't at all sleeping during my whole watch. I was on 6 hrs & off for 2 hours.

Right now it is 4:00 Tuesday afternoon. I tried to go to mass today but after I walked all the way to Fox company the chaplin didn't show up. I am back at my outpost & so is a damn near dead Vietnamese farmer. He stepped on a land mine near his house. He has quite a few holes in him & a lot of his intestines are exposed. The helicopters that are used for evacuation are all out picking up dead & wounded marines from a recon patrol that was ambushed about 2 hrs ago. It will take them another 45 minutes to get up here & by that time the capt'n said he would be dead.

Life is cheap here I hope if I get shot, the helicopter are near enough to pick me up. It had been 14 days since I heard from my girl so the last few days I quit writing her.

I've been pulling my thoughts together. You may not be my girl but you care enough to anser my letter & let me know you appreciate hearing from me. Thats really nice of you.

Hows your beautiful dark stomach Sheri. I'll bet it is going to start getting lighter pretty soon. although it rains over there almost always when it isn't the sun is shining & its making me look like a niger.

I dreampt last night (during the 2 hrs sleep I got) that I got shot four times in the gut that dream was so damn real that when I woke up I was actually surprised I wasn't in a navy hospital.

Have I mentioned that I miss being home lately brother I sure do. I am so bugged about no mail from you know who. That I halfway wish I would get shot up bad enough to be sent home.

But I wouldn't gain much by that because I would have a rough time getting up to your pad to sneak out with one hot doll that I know. *You*

Love Bill